I0666355

The Gym Instructor

First Edition

Christopher Trevor

The Gym Instructor

First Edition

Published by The Nazca Plains Corporation
Las Vegas, Nevada
2007

ISBN: 978-1-887895-44-6

Published by

The Nazca Plains Corporation ®
4640 Paradise Rd, Suite 141
Las Vegas NV 89109-8000

PUBLISHER'S NOTE
The Gym Instructor is a work of fiction created wholly by
Christopher Trevor's imagination. All characters are fictional and
any resemblance to any persons living or deceased is purely
by accident. No portion of this book reflects any real person or
events.

Cover Art, Greasetank
Art Director, Blake Stephens

Acknowledgements

For My Father

(For teaching me to be strong
and to never doubt myself)

The Gym Instructor

Christopher Trevor

Contents

The Gym Instructor

Author's Foreword: I began writing "The Gym Instructor" back in the mid 1990's. As time went on I continued adding to it, seeing as I kept coming up with new ideas for all sorts of trouble that TJ, the lead character for the tale, could find himself falling unwittingly into. That really is at the center of TJ's being, as he unwittingly falls into the clutches of two sadistic yuppies and then later he is just as unwittingly taken prisoner by a psycho cop. At the gym where I worked out at the time was where I first saw TJ the gym instructor. The very handsome guy became the instant inspiration for what I knew would be some sort of hardcore story. With his beguiling good looks and his interesting name, just two initials, I knew I could fashion an erotic tale of some kind around him. He was a tad better than six feet tall, very muscular and well toned with shoulder length well groomed salt and pepper colored hair; GQ cut hair as I would put it. His eyes were piercingly blue, bluer than the ocean on a clear day actually. At the sight of him while I was working out my heart leapt into overdrive. He wore the gym's uniform of red tee shirt, black shorts and high-top sneakers very well, the uniform filling out perfectly his muscula-ture, his well-chiseled body a true work of art. His biceps were the size of bowling balls and I marveled at how the short sleeves of his red tee shirt seemed to be straining around those huge biceps of his. In my opinion there's something very erotic about a guy's muscular arms with the sleeves of his tee shirt just about covering them. His huge barrel-like chest pressed hard against his tee shirt as well, marvelously accenting his huge pecs and big nipples as the tips of those man-sized nips pressed against the tee shirt. I wondered if when TJ was issued his gym uniform, he was purposely given a tee shirt a size or two too small for his glorious muscularity. With all his muscularity I knew that the story I would use him as a model for would be one in which his brute strength was put to a real test. I remember thinking how this extremely handsome gym instructor/personal trainer had the looks of an actor. When I overheard a conversation between TJ and a buddy of his in the locker room and I heard TJ mentioning an acting audition he had to go to and would that buddy cover his client for that day I realized that he was indeed an actor just look-ing for that big break, looking for that role of a life-time to come along. I never had the opportunity to have TJ work for me as a personal trainer, he was always booked weeks in advance. With his looks, charisma and charm I didn't wonder why...

Another time I saw TJ was in the locker room of the gym and it was the sight of him at that moment and the two guys he was talking with that truly caused this story to be born. I had found the idea for a story that I could use the handsome gym instructor/personal trainer as a model for...and lo and behold he had actually unwittingly given me the idea. TJ was standing by his locker talking with two handsome and muscular yuppies. TJ was dressed in his gym shorts, sneakers and sweat socks, his uniform shirt in hand. The two yuppies had just finished working out and showering and they were clad in nothing but their dress socks and white briefs. As TJ leaned against his locker, glorious looking being that he was shirtless for the moment I overheard small tidbits of the conversation he was having with the two scantily clad businessmen. It seemed that, like most people at the gym the two yuppies wanted TJ to be their personal trainer for a few sessions. As I glanced discreetly over at the three men while I was getting dressed after my workout and shower I won-dered just how much TJ would be able to take if the tables were turned and he was the one being made to workout. I did not know the two businessmen's names but somehow I came up with the names Gabriel and Howard. When they finished talking with TJ I heard them thank him and told him that they had better finished getting dressed. TJ looked at his watch and said how he had better get upstairs to the gym, seeing as he had a client waiting. The handsome instructor pulled his tight fitting uniform tee shirt on, shook hands with the two handsome yuppies and exited the locker room. The two yuppies then finished getting dressed and left the locker room as well...

So with all those tidbits of information in mind I created this four part story and I now offer you my revised, re-edited, added onto and subtracted from story, "The Gym Instructor" starring Thomas John, better known as TJ...

My name is Thomas John. My friends and family call me TJ. Recently I wrote in a journal about the time that two very mouthy and extremely full of attitude yuppies named Gabriel and Howard abducted me. Yes, you read that correctly, I was abducted by yuppie scum, two of them to be exact and at my place of work of all things. Actually, to be more precise they abducted me in the locker room of the gym. Can you believe that shit? What a horrid thing to befall a guy huh? I mean, a men's locker room is like church to me, its hallowed ground. It's a place where a guy can trek around naked if he wants and not feel uncomfortable at all. A locker room is a guy's domain. It's a place where even in his most vulnerable, in his underwear and socks maybe, he can still feel secure somehow. What a twisted scene for a want to be actor like me, to be abducted by two yups in the goddamned locker room of the gym I worked in at the time. Those two fuckers...

They forced me to workout to utter and total exhaustion, to really put my muscles to the test and, *and* those two perverts made me shoot my load more times than I can even remember at this point. Thank God for those protein drinks and supplement man's vitamins huh buds? Jeez, by the time Gabriel and Howard were done with me my cock, my balls, my very prostate were aching like nobody's fucking business. Fuckers that they were captured me at closing time at the gym that I used to work at back in New York City. Alright, actually it was sort of my own damned fault because I wanted them to abduct me, maybe, maybe not, sexy bastards that they were, sitting in the locker room after their workouts and showers wearing just their white executive briefs and dark colored dress socks. I've always said that there's something just so fucking sexy about a guy in just his briefs and silky dressy socks. Fucking handsome dudes they were, to say it plainly. I know that I could have stopped them when they grabbed me in the locker room, which as I pointed out was where I found them at closing time that fateful night. What I didn't know was just how much roughing up, sexing down and being worked over I was in for. By the time they had me in their clutches though it was too late to back out. I never thought that two business yuppies could be so fucking sadistic. I always thought that guys in suits, starched white shirts, silk ties, thin socks and leather lace-ups were basically soft and office-driven, total pencil pushers. These two though were anything but. They kept me at the gym all night, all fucking night, forcing me to work real hard, and, forcing me to shoot my damned load over and over again. Being repeatedly milked like that can really make a guy crazy after a while believe me you bud. Bastards that they were they left me roped good and fucking tight to a post in the locker room after they finally left. Two of my work buddies found me there at opening time in the morning and they decided to have some kinky fun with me as well, woe is me. By the time I finally reached home I was way past the point of exhaustion. (I will tell you all about this very shortly in vivid and very intimate detail...) I no longer live in New York City. I now reside in Los Angeles. Before I tell why I'm writing all this let me tell you why I decided to move to LA. Working as a gym instructor/personal trainer is not my life's ambition. I mean, sure, its fun forcing guys through hard workouts, making them grunt and sweat and stink, watching those muscles flex while they struggle with weights, but it really doesn't add up to big dollars when the gym you work for takes a huge chunk of your commission. I want to be an actor. Actually I am an actor. I just need a big break. So, when a friend of mine gave me a tip about a company that was casting for a movie in LA I decided to hightail it out there. It seemed that within a few weeks a movie company was going to be looking for a guy who was about six feet tall with salt and pepper colored hair and blue eyes to play the part of a villain of sorts in an upcoming blockbuster movie. I had all the qualifications physically, so now all I would have to do was make them fall in love with my acting ability. I decided then and there to make it a one-way trip and to move permanently to LA. There really weren't any casting calls or audition calls coming in from companies in New York so I figured that this was an omen and decided to try my luck in LA. I gave the gym manager my letter of resignation he gave me a handshake, a hug and a pat on my sexy ass along with a wish for good luck and I was on my way. I didn't have anything to move because I've always lived in furnished apartments. All I needed to do was pack up all my clothes and I was on my way. When I got to LA I took a furnished room in an apartment building and then looked up the company that was doing the casting for the part I was hoping and praying to land. I called them and a very wispy sounding guy gave me an address to be at in the next three days and the time to be there.

"Is there anything in particular I should be wearing?" I asked him. "Or maybe not wearing?"

"Come as you are," he replied. "If they decide they want you the necessary clothing will be supplied for you."

Before I could say thank you he hung up.

"Rude bastard..." I whispered. "Just as bad as people in New York, jeez, I'll feel right the fuck at home here."

As I was about to close the newspaper I saw an ad for a gym instructor at a gym that wasn't too far from where I was now living. The gym was called "The LA Gym" and I decided to apply for the job, just in case I didn't get the part I didn't want to be stuck living in LA without an income. I figured being that I was a certified gym trainer I would have no problem landing the position. I walked over to the gym to apply in person. I was dressed very spiffily in a blue business suit, a white shirt, red silk tie, black lace-up wingtips and black cotton calf length dress socks, total uniform of the yuppie scum, hardy fucking har and har. Gabriel and Howard would have loved seeing me in my yuppie look I thought musingly as I walked to the gym. When I got there one the instructors directed me to the manager's office. After a pretty lengthy interview the manager of the LA gym told me he was impressed with my résumé and decided to hire me. As we spoke I could not help but notice how he was literally drinking in the sight of me as I sat there with my leg crossed on my knee. The fucking guy's lust was paramount in his eyes. I had closing up duties twice a week. As he told me that I couldn't help but think of Gabriel and Howard. I managed to stifle a chuckle but the gym manager saw my smile and he commented on it by saying that I had a beguiling smile. I thanked him with a smirk and when the interview was over I asked him if there was a bathroom I could use before I headed out on my way. He told me I was welcome to use his private bathroom, pointing to a door in the back of his office. Well, I used the bathroom bud, I also found myself straddled with my back against a urinal, my big hands pressed against the wall, while the gym manager sucked my huge cock as it hung out of the fly opening of my suit pants along with my hairy and sweaty size of kiwi balls. I was balanced up on my tiptoes with my ass in the urinal behind me as the gym manager sucked me for all he was worth; tongue bathed my balls and then scoffed down my ball sap. I grunted and groaned in a man's passion as I fed the guy my creamy and sticky juices. As I zipped up he licked the remains of my manhood off his lips and told me to make sure to be on time for work when my shift started…

On the day that I was to report for the audition at the movie company I woke up extra early so I could go to a car rental place and get a car. The movie company was not in walking distance from where I was living like the gym was and I would need a car for getting around, so until I was able to afford to buy a car I would rent one. After I had finished filling out all the necessary paperwork for renting a car I pulled out of the parking lot in a burgundy colored Cutlass Supreme. It was time for my audition. Being that I had to be at the gym that afternoon for a client's workout and to work into the night I was wearing my gym uniform. It consisted of black shorts; a white tee shirt with the gym logo printed on the center of it, white high-top Reeboks, and black sweat socks scrunched down into the Reeboks. I hummed contentedly to myself as I drove to the movie studio, intent on getting the part in the movie they were casting for. If I landed the part I obviously wouldn't need the job at the gym, I wouldn't have to keep feeding the gym manager my cock and letting him eat my ass like he enjoyed doing, but me, I like to be on the safe side. And like most people, I like having an income, ha, fucking ha. I arrived at the studio at ten AM, parked my car in the visitor's section of the parking lot and walked into the immense building where the studio was. I rode an elevator to the ninth floor and knocked on a door marked "Movie Magic Productions."

"Come in," a male wispy voice called out from the other side of the door. "It's open."

It was the same wispy voice I had heard on the phone when I had called about what or what not to wear. I walked into a reception area where a guy who looked to be about twenty to twenty-two years old was sitting behind an oak desk. He was kind of cute, blond and he was wearing a button down shirt open at the collar.

"Good morning," I said to him and held out my huge ham-like hand. "I'm Thomas John. I'm here to audition for the part you advertised in the newspaper for."

He shook my hand (I quickly took note of the fact that the palm of his hand was sexily moist) and pointed to my other hand. I was holding a brown envelope, which contained my résumé and headshots.

"Oh yes, my résumé and headshots..." I said, holding the envelope out for him to take.

"Have a seat," he said to me blandly.

"Thanks," I said and sat down in a nearby chair. He opened the envelope, pulled out my résumé and one of my headshots and stood up.

"I'll be right back Mr. John," he said and swished into an office behind him, closing the door as he went.

I crossed one leg over my knee and waited anxiously. A few minutes later the blond guy came out, leaving the door to the office behind him open.

"You can go in," he said to me, looking at me the way a vampire would look at a milk-white neck when it was time to feed. "Mr. Walker will see you now."

I stood up, said thank you, and walked briskly into the office. There were cameras, camcorders, VCR's, and all kinds of movie equipment all set up all over the place.

"Ah, Mr. John, thank you, thank you for coming by today," a short and stocky looking guy said to me as he approached me from across the room. "Please excuse the mess but we've been so busy here lately. I'm Chester, Chester Walker."

I shook hands with him and it actually felt like a claw had grabbed my hand.

"I must say that you do indeed meet the description of the type of gentleman we advertised for, but I'm sad to say that we can't use you," Mr. Walker said dejectedly.

"Huh? What?" I asked feeling totally dumbfounded. "Why not?"

"Well, because the part was filled yesterday," he explained. "I'm so sorry…"

"But your ad said auditions were being held today Sir," I said, feeling confused and angry now.

"I know, and I'm sure many more men just like you, many more handsome men just like you will be showing up and I will have to turn them away also," he went on. "You see, quite by chance, a messenger had come by yesterday to drop off a package and he fit the description for the guy we were looking for as well. It turned out he was a want to be actor, he had an impressive résumé just like yours and the rest as they say is history."

I thanked Mr. Walker for his time, asked that he please keep my name and picture on file and walked angrily and dejectedly out of his office. I didn't even acknowledge the wispy receptionist's good-bye as I stomped past him and out of the building. I could not believe my rotten fucking luck. I got in my car, punched the steering wheel, started it up and headed back toward my apartment, not knowing at that moment that I would not be getting there, no, I would not be getting there for some time bud. I got on a highway that would get me to my apartment a few minutes sooner. I really just wanted to be alone so that I could sulk in anger by myself. I angrily wrapped my fingers around the steering wheel and pressed my big foot against the accelerator pedal. Fuck it all I thought miserably. I had uprooted my whole life on the hope and the chance of getting that damned part. I was so preoccupied with my thoughts that I didn't realize how fast I was driving as the anger welled in me more and more. But then, as I was driving I heard a police car siren directly behind me and then suddenly, a blaring voice calling out over a loudspeaker/ intercom of sorts said, "Burgundy Cutlass, pull over to the side of the road and stop your vehicle." Realizing it was me the cop behind me was paging I immediately did as I was told, wondering why the fuck I was being pulled over, as if this day hadn't been bad enough already. What I didn't know was just how very bad the day was going to become. The cop stopped his patrol cruiser behind me and slowly got out. As he approached my car I saw in my rear-view mirror that he was extremely tall. His uniform was all dark blue along with black shiny rubber boots that came up to just under his knees. He was clean-cut and I guessed his hair to be blond under his cap. With his fair complexion it seemed reasonable to assume his hair was blond. When he was standing next to my car I rolled down the window and he leaned in, looking at me intently. The scent of his cologne mixed with a slight hint of sweat filled my nostrils. His eyes, like mine, were as blue as the ocean. At the sight and scent of him my heart leapt in my chest. "Is, is there a problem Officer?" I asked him, feeling nervous and lustful at the same time.

I saw that his nametag said "Ryder."

"Going a bit fast there weren't you buddy?" he asked me and I could feel his breath on my face, he was leaning in that close to me.

"Was I?" I asked him. "I uh, I was only doing fifty Officer."

"The speed limit is thirty-five," he said sternly and stood up straight so that his crotch was staring me in the face. "Could you please step out of the car?"

I did as he asked, stepping slowly out of my Cutlass. He was better than six feet tall that was for damn sure, just a bit taller than me actually.

"Can I see your license please?" he asked me.

I took my wallet out of my back pocket and extracted my driver's license. I handed it to him.

"So, you're from New York eh Mr. John?" the cop asked me, suddenly grinning meanly.

"Yes, uh, I'm new to Los Angeles and I guess I didn't know about the speed limits here," I said sheepishly as my cock was betraying me and getting hard in my shorts.

He nodded slowly and slipped my driver's license into his pants pocket.

"When were you planning on applying for a California driver's license Mr. John?" Officer Ryder asked me.

"Well, I had a job interview today so I figured I would get to that real soon Sir," I replied dumbly.

"A real New Yorker eh?" he asked me with that evil grin again on his handsome face.

"Yes, a native I suppose you could say Sir," I responded, starting to feel slightly nervous, seeing as he had placed my driver's license in his pants pocket and didn't seem about to give it back to me.

As we stood facing each other cars were passing by every few moments and some were slowing down so the driver's could see what was happening. Just like in New York people were damned curious over another person's misfortune.

"Mr. John, I want you to walk a straight line for me," Officer Ryder said to me, backing up a few steps. "Walk toward me, nice and slow, nice and straight."

"I'm not intoxicated," I said and began walking toward him.

"Just have to make sure," he said. "Also, while I'm talking to you I want your hands raised over your head where I can see them."

"Hey come on now, I'm not armed or anything…" I began.

"Do as you are told Mr. John!!" the cop roared at me, drawing attention to himself.

I instantly put my hands up over my head, a look of fear suddenly etched on my mug.

"Y-you can see I'm not armed," I said to him as I walked a straight line toward him. "I mean, where could I possibly hide a gun in what I'm wearing?"

"Yes, that's for sure," he said, leering at me now. "But, I think I'll search you anyway, never know where someone may stash drugs nowadays. Turn back and lean on your car with your legs spread Mr. John."

My heart thundered in my chest at what I knew was coming but again, I did as I was told, almost dreading what was coming next. Officer Ryder squatted down behind me and ran his big hands slowly over the sides of my shorts. Slowly, he moved his hands under my crotch and gave my hefty balls a squeeze and a hard tug through my shorts. I yelped slightly and then he moved his hands over the front of my shorts. If he noticed my boner he didn't make mention of it, even though the palm of his hand had roamed slowly over it, twice actually. I was so lost in what was happening that I could have sworn he gave my hard cock a squeeze through my shorts. When I heard him sniffing heartily I knew he was stealing sniffs at my ass. He then donned thin latex gloves, reached under my shorts, his two fingers stealthily moving along my ass cheek and he told me to remain perfectly still. I clenched my teeth as his fingers probed deep in my hole, searching me back there for drugs, a favorite place of many a drug runner when it came to hiding the goods. I grunted loudly as he seemed to be having a grand old time digging for gold or drugs in my stink hole. He found none, obviously and the sound of the gloves being snapped off his hands filled the air it seemed. Next, he stood up and towered behind me and ran those big hands of his over my chest, making like he was feeling for any padding that I might have under my shirt, another place where illegal drugs could have been hidden. He deliberately found my big nipples under my tee shirt and gave them a hard squeeze, getting another slight yelp out of me.

"Lady tits," he whispered and went on with his probing search.

He moved his big hands down my sides, patting me down as he went, his touch making me breathless. Then, satisfied that I wasn't armed, at least not with a gun, he stepped away from me and told me to turn around and face him, with my hands in the air. Miserably, I again did as I was told.

"Nope, no gun and you don't seem to be intoxicated," he said to me, both of us glancing down at the ground where his used latex gloves were.

My ass innards were still feeling it from when his fingers had just a few moments ago dug in them.

"But, you're still in a shit load of trouble for speeding," he went on.

"You uh, couldn't give me a break this time eh Officer?" I asked him. "I mean, being new to LA and all."

He seemed to consider my request and then pointed to my tee shirt with the gym logo on it.

"You work at the LA gym?" he asked me.

"Yes, I'm a personal trainer there," I replied.

He nodded, seeming to consider my request for a break.

"You workout there as well?" he then asked.

"I guess I will, eventually," I said.

He smiled fiendishly and placed his hand on his baton, which was hanging off the side of his belt, right next to his revolver.

"Are you a bad ass personal trainer Mr. John?" Officer Ryder asked me with a smirk. "A New Yorker like you probably is."

"No Sir, not a bad ass at all...just a trainer trying to make a living..." I replied with the utmost respect.

"Guy like you can probably endure a shit load of abuse eh Mr. John?" the cop asked me, sounding very wicked now. "You uh, ever have been down in the California valleys Mr. John?"

Smiling, he pointed at me with a long finger, his other hand still resting on his baton.

"No, as I said I'm new to LA and all..." I replied, my arms starting to get tired from being held up so long.

"Maybe you should see one of the valleys Mr. John..." Officer Ryder mused. "Maybe you could get that break you asked me for a few moments ago. I have a farmhouse down there in the woods, all by itself Mr. John. New Yorker like you never saw a place like it I'll bet. Maybe a couple of cop buddies of mine and I could give you hands on guided tour of the place and the woods around it. Maybe you should take a ride with us there...*right now...maybe...*"

"Uh, I have to work today at the gym...maybe another time..." I stammered nervously, wondering what this muscle bound, overly tall cop had in mind for me and just where he was going with all this talk of farmhouses and woods.

Suddenly, his baton was off his belt and in his hand. He quickly swung the wooden instrument sharply at my legs, moving with the speed of lightning. His baton connected hard with my naked legs, literally knocking me off my feet.

"UHHHNNNFFFFF..." I gasped in surprise as I landed at Officer Ryder's booted feet. "Hey, now hold on here Sir..."

"I don't like resistors Mr. John," the cop said, stepping over me, pressing a foot into the small of my back, and leaning over me with a lot of weight behind me.

"UUUUHHHHH!!!!" I panted.

He yanked my arms behind me and before I even realized it my hands were cuffed behind my back at the wrists.

"Hey, what is this man?" I ranted angrily now. "All you have to do is write me out a damned ticket for exceeding the speed limit and I'll pay it..."

"I told you what you're going to do Mr. John..." the cop said sternly and grabbed a handful of my salt and pepper colored shoulder length hair. "...a nice trip to the valley...where my damned farmhouse is..."

He roughly and most savagely yanked me to my feet, pulling me up by the handful of my hair in his fist.

"AAAAYYYYRRRRR!!!!" I screamed in a man's agony, my voice echoing in the air as he hauled me to my feet.

I stood there against my rental car, panting for breath, gasping in pain as he placed his baton back on his belt.

"I'll call in to the station to tell the dispatcher I'm going off duty...then I'll summon my two buddies to meet us here. They have today off and nothing to do...lucky I caught you speeding eh Mr. John?" Officer Ryder said to me as the pain in my legs and head throbbed. "One of them will drive your car to the valley while you, me, and my other buddy will ride in my patrol car...

Looking at me he snickered meanly.

"Wh-what is so funny?" I asked him miserably, the pain in my legs and head growing worse each second.

"You're going to ride in the trunk of my cruiser Mr. John..." the cop said fiendishly. "Fucking big pile of shit New Yorker you are...you're about to be reduced to a beat up pile of shit, we're going to turn you into road kill. When my two buddies and I get done with you there won't be any New Yorker left to send home to your friends or family..."

"Y-you can't mean this..." I whispered in total terror. "This is entrapment, not to mention kidnapping…"

"Oh yes I can do it, and I am doing it…starting now Mr. John…" the cop said sternly, grabbed a handful of my tee shirt and yanked me away from my rental car. "Move your ass fucker, get over to my patrol car…*walk!!!*"

He shoved me toward his car, letting go of my tee-shirt, causing me to almost lose my balance again. I turned and looked at him in disbelief for a moment, anger etched on my face as well, then did as he said, walking on wobbly feet toward his patrol cruiser. Being handcuffed there wasn't much I was going to be able to do to defend myself against this obviously insane cop. He walked closely behind me, making sure I would not try to make a break for it. But then again, where would I manage to go with my hands cuffed behind me?

"Okay, stand right there and don't move…" the cop ordered when I was standing next to his patrol car. "And if you want to make it through this day you won't utter a goddamned sound…"

I grimaced miserably and looked longingly at the few cars that were passing on the parkway beside us as he pulled his hand-held dispatch radio receiver from his car.

"Hey Molly girl, this is Ryder…you there honey?" Officer Ryder said into the small hand-held device.

A few seconds later a female voice emanated from the radio in the car.

"Yeah Ryder, I'm here," the woman named Molly responded. "What can I do for you cutie?"

Ryder smiled like a schoolboy before responding to her affectionate word of "cutie" for him.

"Listen Molly, I'm not feeling all that well honey…" Ryder responded, looking at me and giving my tee shirt a tug in the front, showing his possession of me as he did so. "Stomach is acting up on me real bad. Must be something I ate with breakfast earlier. I'm goin' to go off duty. You got someone you can dispatch on my patrol for today?"

"Sure honey, I'll call Henderson…" Molly said. "He's doing a double shift today after all. You feel better now, hear?"

"Yeah, I hear honey, and thanks, thanks so much…" Ryder said with an awful looking grin on his face.

"Will you be in tomorrow cutie?" Molly asked Ryder before signing off.

"That depends honey," Ryder responded, looking at me with death glaring in his eyes. "That depends on how I feel tomorrow…"

With that Ryder moved a hand in my long hair, tugged it gently and he clicked off his radio.

"I do not believe this is happening…" I mumbled, looking down at the ground.

"Easy Mr. John, easy now…" Ryder said stroking my long salt and pepper colored hair. "If you make it through this little harrowing experience you're about to have we'll let you go, if not, well, that's just how it goes I suppose."

I looked up at him miserably as he smiled from ear to ear and pulled a cellular phone from his uniform pants pocket. He dialed a number and put the phone to his ear. As he waited for whomever he was calling to answer I looked out at the parkway, looking at the cars that past every few moments. I was being abducted by a damned psycho cop. Who in any of those cars would come to my aid if I yelled out for help? My captor being a cop no one in his or her right mind would believe me. What a fucked up situation I was in…

"Hey Alex, its Ryder…" the cop said enthusiastically into his cellular phone. "How's it goin' man?"

Ryder paused to listen and smiled again from ear to fucking ear.

"That's right bud, I told you, I fucking told you I would call you guys if, and only if I managed to find us a chicken for today," Ryder said gleefully, hooking a big hand tightly around one of my muscular arms and holding it tight. "Well guess what the fuck man…I am at this very goddamned moment holding onto a cuffed, muscular, hot looking, and scared to shit New York guy. *And I do mean hot looking Alex my man.* Fucking guy is built like a bull. Picked him up right out here on the highway just a few minutes ago for speeding. He's a fucking personal trainer of all things…the kind of fucker you and that psycho Ronald would love to get your filthy paws on. Way I figure it we'll take this stack of New York shit out to that big mangy farmhouse out in the woods that I inherited from my good for nothing dead uncle…looks like my uncle was good for something after all huh?"

Ryder again paused to listen, still smiling from ear to ear. I was shaking in my sneakers as he spoke to whoever Alex was.

"Can't just bring him there just like that Alex…" Ryder said, squeezing my arm tighter. "That's why I need you and Ronald out here. I need one of you to drive his car while I drove my patrol cruiser out there. Going to put the New York fucker in the trunk…"

I rolled my head and eyes in utter disbelief and fear over

this twisted turn of events as Officer Ryder snickered into the phone.

"Yeah, I know, get started really working the poor fuck by making him sweat real well for us..." Ryder said. "I'm two miles down on route thirty nine. How soon can you two sick fucks be here?"

Ryder listened, squeezing my muscular arm tighter yet as he did.

"Okay, I'll be here waiting for you...don't worry I'll find a way to kill twenty minutes or so," Ryder said to his friend Alex, looking around at the same time. "There's a rest stop just off the road here, real mangy place that no one uses anymore. I'll take my New York boy in the men's room and...well, you know what I'll do..."

Ryder laughed insanely this time...

"Okay man, see you here soon..." he said and clicked off his cellular phone.

"You, you can't mean this..." I said, sounding like a captured super hero from a bad comic book, but shaking in total fear nonetheless.

Ryder didn't say a word in response. He simply looked at me again with death showing in his eyes. Just from that look I knew that he meant every word of what he was planning for me. Good God almighty, what had I stumbled into this time??? The cop slipped his cellular phone back into his pants pocket, and still holding my arm tightly in his firm vise-like grasp he walked me over to the rest stop on the side of the road. We walked into the deserted, foul smelling bathroom and Ryder locked the door behind us.

"You're in for the fucking ride of your life Scumbag..." Ryder said, slamming me bodily and meanly into a tile wall, letting go of my arm as he flung me forward.

"UHHHHNNNFFFF!!!" I whimpered and slid to the filthy floor on my knees.

"On your feet Mr. John..." Ryder ordered and I quickly did as I was told.

But the second I was on my feet Ryder's baton was in his hand. He again swung it at my legs, connected hard just below my knees, and knocked me off my feet again. I landed this time with a terrible thud flat on my ass.

"UHHHNNFFFF!!!" I gasped.

"I said to get up on your feet asshole!!" Ryder shouted angrily at me.

"SH-shit man..." I stammered, and slowly pulled myself to my feet again as Ryder placed his baton back on his belt again.

"I'm not your man Mr. John; I am Officer Ryder, your worst fucking nightmare brought to life!" Ryder said through clenched teeth, grabbed a handful of my tee shirt, yanked me forward and slammed me against the tile wall again. "And for the time we'll be spending together you will address me as such!! *Is that clear asshole?*"

"Y-yes Officer Ryder, it's clear..." I replied shakily, cowering against the wall he had just flung me against.

"Damn, you're fucking hot man, what a fucking total stroke of luck..." Ryder said, pulled me to him by my tee shirt and clamped his mouth down real hard on mine.

"RRRMMMFFFF..." I gasped as Ryder savagely sucked my tongue into his mouth.

The way he sucked my tongue it felt as if he was going to literally rip it from my mouth. I had visions of him doing that and leaving me there in the roadside stinking bathroom to bleed and choke to death on my own blood. When he stopped kissing me and looked at me insanely I felt as if I had just been given the kiss of death.

"Got a job for you Mr. John..." Ryder said mockingly, his fingers roaming over his shiny belt police issued buckle.

Moments later I was on my knees in front of the monster-sized cop, licking his belt buckle with the tip of my tongue, shining it up for him.

"That's it you asshole, lick that buckle clean for me...and when you're done with that I'll have you clean up my badge for me..." Officer Ryder laughed, caressing the side of my face with his baton.

Every time he brought his baton close to my trembling lips I kissed it, gave it a few sucks as he prodded my mouth with it, and then quickly resumed licking his belt buckle. The taste of metal assaulted my taste buds but I was in no goddamned position to complain about what the big cop was demanding of me. I stole glances at the big plumpness in Officer Ryder's uniform pants. It looked like a horse-sized cock he had in those pants. Despite my fear my mouth salivated for his cock but I simply went on licking his belt buckle. A few minutes or so later I was back on my feet, standing very close to the cop, leaning my head forward, licking his badge clean for him, shining it up as I had done with his belt buckle. Officer Ryder stood practically at attention, rubbing my upper back with his baton, slapping me lightly with it over my wide as a doorway shoulders. I fleetingly thought about kneeing him in the nuts and making a run for it, but he would surely bash me with his baton long before I was even a few scant inches away from him.

"Man oh man Mr. John, I would not want to be in your place for all the damned money in the world…" Ryder said, actually sounding like he felt sorry for me. "You are not going to believe half of what my two buddies and I are going to do to you when we get you to my farm…"

Ryder then gripped the back of my big bull-sized neck and stroked my long hair almost lovingly as I went on licking his badge.

"Yeah, that's it Mr. John, lick that fucking badge of mine… get it real shiny for me…" Ryder said breathlessly as if I were sucking his cock. "Fucking bad assed cop like me needs his badge good and shiny looking…"

I knew at some point that I would be chowing down on his horse-sized cop cock. At that moment I wasn't sure if he was holding out on me because he wanted me to anticipate sucking his meat while he fed it to me…or if he was just enjoying the mounting excitement he was feeling at his capture of me. When I was done licking his badge clean it was so damned shiny I was able to see my tongue reflected in it. He let go of the back of my neck, and without being told to do so I leaned my face toward his nametag and kissed it twice, whispering the name of my captor in between kissing his badge. Ryder snickered meanly and squeezed my right nipple good and fucking hard through my tee shirt with his thumb and first two fingers, really twisting and pinching the fuck out of it.

"AAAYYYRRRR!!!!" I screamed in a man's pain, my loud voice bouncing off the tile walls of the foul smelling men's room.

I tried to pull my nipple out of Ryder's grasp but he held on tight, really making me squirm and do a dance of pain on my wobbly feet.

"AAAAAYYYYYRRRR SHIT, pl-please Officer Ryder..." I gasped as he pulled super hard on my poor nipple, making me take a few small steps toward him.

Then, once again Ryder's mouth was clamped down hard on mine, sucking the very fuck out of my tongue as he continued squeezing, twisting, and out-rightly torturing my poor right nipple.

"RRRRMMMFFFF..." I wailed as the cop painfully kissed me.

"You need to piss asshole?" he asked me when he released my mouth the second time.

"N-no Officer Ryder..." I stammered softly, my tongue feeling awful, my nipple smarting. "I don't have to piss..."

"Well I do..." Ryder said snidely, reaching for his pants zipper and pulling it down. "Get back on your knees asshole; you're going to be my toilet. I'll be damned if I'll use one of the germs infested urinals or stalls in this filthy shit house..." As Ryder prepared to take his horse-sized cock out of his uniform pants I slowly made my way back down to my knees in front of the cop, dying to see his meat, but not overly anxious at the prospect of scoffing down his piss. Ryder pulled his pants zipper down real slow, making me anticipate what his horse cock would look like. He then reached into the fly opening of his uniform pants, past his underpants, and brought out a real fat, thick, Irish sausage sized cock. It was humungous, totally meaty. He dangled it in front of my face, twisting and squeezing the dowel, putting his dick slit close to my quivering lips.

"Open wide asshole..."Ryder exclaimed demandingly. "I have a nice stout sized mess of cop piss to unload on you..."

I automatically did as I was told. The sight of his manhood left me speechless let me tell you. I tilted my head back and Ryder placed just the crown of his immense cock into my mouth. He began pissing...and I began dutifully gulping it down...it tasted rancid and vile.

"Ahhhh, now that really feels good..." Ryder exclaimed as his bladder drained into my mouth. "Haven't taken a piss all fucking day. And may God help you if you lose a drop of it asshole..." When he was halfway done he stopped pissing for a moment or two so I could catch my breath...but then he quickly slid the crown of his cock back into my mouth to finish the job. I drank every despicable tasting drop of his cop piss, not losing any of it. When he was done he packed his giant manhood back into his uniform pants and zipped up as I knelt there with my head bowed, licking my pissy tasting lips.

"On your feet asshole..."Ryder said sternly. "Its time for us to get moving. My buddies will be here pretty soon now."

I got myself to my feet and stood in front of the big cop, every part of me utterly trembling.

"L-look Officer..." I stuttered. "Can't we work this out somehow? I mean, none of this is really necessary..."

He smiled fiendishly and without warning or hesitation he gave me a hard resounding rap across my face, sending me spiraling around and around and against a wall.

"UHHHNNNFFFF..." I gasped; the wind literally knocked out of me, this time my head spinning.

"Some New Yorker..." Ryder said sarcastically, walked over to me, and took me by my upper arm. "No wonder you moved out here, you couldn't weather New York City. From this moment on you'll speak only when I give you permission to. And God help you if you fuck up on that order. Come on asshole..."

I walked on wobbly feet out of the men's room with Officer Ryder. As we were walking back over to his police cruiser I saw another police car pull up behind his.

"Perfect, they're here..."Ryder whispered, squeezing my arm tight, inflicting pain as my head still spun from the rap I had been dealt moments ago.

Two guys, not in police regalia emerged from the car as Ryder and I walked over to them.

"Hey you guys..." Ryder said happily, almost sounding normal and shook hands with the two men. "So glad you two could make the party. This is our guest of honor here. Thomas John, you asshole, meet my two best buddies in the entire world, Alex and Ronald.

"Good to meet you man, I'm Alex..." the five foot nine inch tall guy with the wavy brown hair and light brown eyes said to me.

"And I'm Ronald..." the over six foot tall hulk of a muscle guy with dark hair and dark eyes said to me.

"Say hello asshole..." Ryder ordered.

"G-good to meet both of you..." I stammered. "I guess..."

They were both dressed in worn looking jeans, work boots, and mussed up tee shirts.

"He would shake hands but unfortunately I had to cuff him," Ryder said, holding tightly to my arm. "Fucker was speeding and needed slowing down..."

The two men laughed mockingly and Ryder moved me toward the back of his car.

"All right you guys, lets do this fast..."Ryder said. "Wait till there are no cars around and then help me load this pile of shit into the trunk. Don't want any witnesses okay? We wouldn't want anyone claiming police brutality, ha, ha!"

"Shit man, the fucking lug looks real scared Ryder..." Alex said as Ryder opened the trunk of his patrol car.

"As he should..." Ryder said with a grin, looking around to double check that there were no cars on the road at the moment. "Fucking guy has no idea whatsoever what he's in for when we get him to my farm... Okay, the coast is, as they say, clear guys...hoist that load of shit in here...fast..."

Ryder pushed the spare tire in the trunk to the back of the enclosure as Alex and Ronald hoisted me off the ground by my arms and legs. They loaded me into the trunk like so much baggage and watched as I shivered in mortal fear, pulling myself into a somewhat fetal position of sorts.

"Will he be able to breathe in there?" Alex asked Ryder, sounding genuinely concerned.

"Yeah, there are air holes in the sides of the lid..." Ryder responded. "I've been planning something like this for a long fucking time now..."

With that Ryder slammed the trunk shut, plunging me into total darkness.

"Okay, Alex, you drive the guy's car," I heard Ryder say. "Keys are still in the ignition. Ronald, you'll have to drive your patrol car behind me beside Alex, got it?"

"Yeah, sure..." Ronald said.

"Let's get going..."Alex said anxiously.

"When we're halfway there we'll stop along side the road to stretch our legs...and for a little fun, if you catch my drift..." Ryder said.

As I cowered there in the trunk I felt the movement of Ryder climbing into the driver's seat of the patrol cruiser. Seconds later we were moving... My tears of fear flowed down my cheeks as I shivered and quaked in fear and total agony in that damned trunk...

While the car was moving toward Ryder's farm I thought back on my first experience of abduction...the one I mentioned earlier which was at the hands of those two mouthy and full of attitude yuppies, Gabriel and Howard...

It had been my turn to work the late night and close and lock up the gym for the night. So, at ten o'clock I walked down to the men's locker room to begin making sure there were no members left in the gym. (The gym officially closes at ten PM on weeknights.) Dressed in a pair of black shorts, a red tee shirt, (with the gym logo stenciled on the front of it) a pair of Reebok sneakers and black cotton calf length sweat socks I walked into the men's locker room. As I entered I heard voices and sure enough, there were two yuppies sitting there on a bench between the rows of lockers having a conversation about big business. I had seen those two yups earlier upstairs in the gym while they were working out. They were dressed in just their executive briefs and dress socks. Obviously they had showered and had paused in getting dressed to sit down and have an office conversation, on my time… I slowly made my way over to them.

"Hey guys, good evening," I said politely. "The gym is closed. You'll have to finish getting dressed and leave now."

They both looked up at me and from the looks on their handsome faces it was obvious they were a tad rattled at having been interrupted.

"Are you the owner of the gym?" one of them asked me. "Well, no, I'm not," I replied, a bit taken aback by the guy's attitude.

"Or, are you the gym manager?" the other yuppie asked me, him also sounding nasty.

"No!" I replied somewhat loudly. "It's just my job to make sure that everyone has left the gym before I lock the place up for the night."

They both stood up, looking me up and down, seeming to be devouring me with their eyes.

"So, what you're saying is that we're the only two people in the gym right now TJ?" the first yuppie asked me, staring at my nametag which was pinned to my shirt.

"Yes, we are, so you two will have to leave…" I said them, all of a sudden not sounding all that sure of myself.

"Did you workout today TJ?" the second yuppie asked me.

"No," I responded. "Gym instructors and personal trainers

can only use the facilities during their non-working hours.

"So, if you were to workout now no one would know, right?" the second yuppie asked me.

"I-I suppose not," I replied, not knowing what the sadistic fuck had in mind for me.

Their better than thou attitude really irked the fuck out of me but God; they both looked so damned sexy standing there in their briefs and dress socks. The first guy was about my height with brown hair, brown eyes and a pretty muscular body. I had to wonder how he was able to squeeze all that musculature comfortably into his business suit. Standing there he was wearing brown calf length silk socks. The second guy was slightly shorter with light brown hair, green eyes, and a very muscular body. Actually he was built like a goddamned bull and like his buddy I had to wonder just how comfortable he felt from nine to five wedged in a suit, a choker of a tie and thin socks. Speaking of his socks the ones he was wearing were black, knee length, OTC (over the calf) as executives such as himself called them. They were both wearing white briefs and to say it pretty plainly they were both pretty plumped up in those briefs. It looked to me like Ringling Brothers had decided to pitch tents in these two yuppie's briefs, hardy har and har.

"Look, you guys really have to finish getting dressed and leave now," I said again, ignoring their questions about my not having worked out that day.

They each took a step toward me. I never in a million years thought that two guys could look so threatening in their briefs and silk socks, but these two did; they sure as hell did bud. The first yuppie squeezed one of my upper arms.

"I don't know TJ," he said to me in a silly sounding tone.

"Seems to me this arm is kind of soft. A big ol' gym instructor like you should be rock fucking solid. Wouldn't you agree Howard?"

"I sure as shit would," the second yuppie said, hooking a hand around my other arm.

Then, with total suddenness they twisted my arms forward and then yanked them up behind me, twisting them hard as they went.

"UUNNGHHHH!!!" I grunted, totally staggered. "*What the fucking hell?!?*"

"You need a good hard workout TJ my boy," the first yuppie said to me, sounding like he was telling an office underling something. "And we're going to make sure you get it. Funny how we were just a few minutes ago saying how we would love to really work a gym trainer over big time…just to see if one of you guys can take it as well as dish it out on clients like us. Well, it looks to us like we're going to get our chance TJ, because here you are."

I struggled like a captured marine in their grasps but it was no fucking use. I could not pull free of their strong grips. And to tell it like it is, inwardly I didn't want to escape from them. As I said, they were both so damned sexy.

"He isn't all that rough now huh Gabriel?" the second yuppie asked his buddy.

"No Howard, he isn't," Gabriel replied. "And this should calm him down a lot."

With that, the guy named Gabriel kneed me hard in the balls.

"OOOOOFFF!" was all I could say as pain shot through me and the wind was knocked out of me. "Th-that's a shitty thing to do to a guy..."

Moments later they had my hands securely tied behind my back with their silk neckties of all things.

"L-look guys..." I began sheepishly, my balls still aching from the blow they'd been dealt. "I-I just work here. I'm just doing my goddamn job!! Do you think I really care if you leave or not?"

"Shut the fuck up TJ, or I'm going to cram one of my stinking socks into your mouth," Gabriel said to me harshly.

I instantly clammed up. Sexy as he was I didn't feel like tasting his smelly socks...

"Now, here's what we're going to do," Gabriel said with a fiendish looking glint in his eyes. "We're all going upstairs to the gym. TJ, you're going to workout. You are going to workout past excess and past exhaustion! You are going to workout till you're swathed in sweat and gasping like a crazy person. You are going to workout till you don't know your name."

I stared at him dumbfounded...

"Now, to add to all this merriment," Gabriel went on. "For every moment you falter we'll rap and thrash you hard with our designer leather belts on the tenderest and sweetest parts of that muscle body of yours TJ. In between working out we'll allow you to jack off. Actually I plan to milk your balls dry TJ ol' TJ. And believe me you muscle head, by the time you're done working out and flogging your dong you'll be more exhausted and spent than ever before in your life!!"

"Milk him dry..." Howard laughed. "Shit Gabriel, you really do come up with the nuttiest things to do to a poor sap of a guy..."

Listening to them was giving me a boner already. Gabriel propped one of his socked feet up on the bench that we were all standing next to and asked me in a snidely tone of voice what I thought of their wicked plans for me. I gulped hard and instead of responding to him verbally I knelt down and licked his brown socked foot like crazy. I slid my tongue along the top of his foot, kissed it a few times and then kissed my way up his socked calf and back down again. I puckered my lips against his toes and licked them like crazy. The odor of Gabriel's sock was pungent and musty, it invaded my nostrils as I licked and licked his socked foot. The two yuppies howled with sadistic sounding laughter and a few minutes later they were both dressed in shorts, tee shirts, and sneakers. With my hands still bound behind me I walked between them to the elevator that would take us to the gym floor. They each wielded a leather belt in their hands. At the elevator Gabriel pressed the button. The elevator was slow in arriving.

"Lick my goddamned socks while we're waiting for the elevator TJ," Gabriel ordered.

I quickly dropped to my knees and lowered my head to Gabriel's feet. Before I started licking I dutifully kissed the tops of his brown socks all around his iron-like calves. I then licked his stinking socks like I couldn't get enough of them. I drooled over the sides of them and quickly sucked up my saliva. I again kissed his socks up and down and licked at them some more, truly savoring the taste of his sneaker and silk sock odor as they mixed together.

"Looks to me like we've got ourselves a real obedient and submissive boy here," Gabriel said to Howard.

Howard responded by giving my raised sexy butt cheeks two hard swats with his leather belt.

"OOOWWWWCCHHHH!!!" I yelled.

The elevator doors opened and Gabriel yanked me quickly and roughly to my feet by a handful of my hair.

"AAAAARRRRRRR!!!! Looks like the workout is starting already huh??!!" I said to Gabriel as he and Howard pushed me meanly into the elevator.

"Like I said TJ my boy, you're going to workout like never before!" Gabriel said authoritatively, taking me by one arm.

We rode the elevator to the third floor which was where all the Nautilus and Cybex machines were located. Included on the third floor were free weights and rubber mats where gym members could do sit-ups, crunches, stretches, and whatever else needed to be done during a workout. We exited the elevator with Gabriel and Howard each holding one of my upper arms tightly. I realized that, in a way, I had been kidnapped. At that thought my cock grew even harder in my shorts.

"I'm going to untie your hands TJ ol' boy," Gabriel said to me. "But don't even consider going anywhere. Remember what I said about our leather belts.

"Y-yes Sir, I remember," I replied as the sadistic yuppie untied my hands.

It was not said but it sure seemed obvious that we were all on the same page where this fantasy being acted out was concerned. Was Gabriel kidding when he told me not consider going anywhere as he untied my hands. Once my hands were freed I could have swatted those two damned yuppies out of my face like flies and been on my way home. But like Gabriel had said, they had a real submissive boy in me and inwardly I truly loved this.

The workout began with me lifting two thirty-pound dumbbells alternately. I held a dumbbell in each of my big hands, stood well positioned with my knees slightly bent in front of a full-length mirror and lifted the weights as Gabriel and Howard stood by watching me, their belts in hand.

"Unnnnfffff!!!" I grunted as I lifted and lifted the weights, the muscles in my huge biceps flexing and straining as I did so.

"You're going to do five sets of twelve reps TJ my boy," Gabriel said. "That's sixty reps altogether. After that warm-up your arms should be feeling real good."

When I had reached forty reps I began to falter. Even the strongest and most muscular of guys weaken after constant sets upon sets of repeated weight lifting. I was by then lifting the weights slower with each rep.

"Ahhhhh…I-I can't…" I moaned throatily.

Howard quickly gave my butt a fast crack with his belt as Gabriel whacked the backs of my thighs with his belt.

"UNNNGGGGHHHH!!!" I said miserably, my teeth clenched and lifted the weights faster, those two whacks having been successful in spurring me on.

"There you go TJ ol' boy, a second fucking wind for you," Gabriel teased me. "Just keep in mind that in between some of the intense exercises we force you through you'll be allowed to jack off. Isn't that great?"

"Yeah, I'm feeling real cheered up already," I replied sarcastically.

I looked around at all the machines I would most likely be using and tried to calculate how many times I would probably be forced to jack off. The number was astounding and my prostate ached just at the prospect of it all.

"God almighty, you really are planning to milk me dry by the time this shit is over!!" I shouted.

The two men (my captors) laughed and whacked my ass again with their belts, just for sadistic fun. The stinging sounds echoed maddeningly through the gym. I grunted angrily as I lifted and lifted and lifted the weights. When I had completed my sixty reps I dropped the weights to the rubber covered floor and stretched my aching arms to relieve the pain in them. Gabriel and Howard had me flex my huge biceps muscles and they ran their hands lovingly and greedily over them, squeezing them hard.

"Feels good TJ," Gabriel said. "Feels real fucking good."

Howard had one hand on my ass as he felt up my other biceps. He grabbed a handful of my ass cheek and squeezed my biceps harder yet. My cock grew to gargantuan proportions in my shorts. I was ready to shoot a load buds. Somehow the combination of all of it, being abducted, being forced to workout by two insane yuppies and then made to crank my crank was sending me over the top. I was building a load in my balls like never before in my life.

"Okay TJ, reach for your meat pole and let's see you shoot that load of yours!" Gabriel said. "The way you're all chubbed up in your shorts I get the feeling you could shoot enough to choke a horse with…"

I glanced angrily at him in the mirror I was still facing, pushed my shorts aside, reached into my briefs and yanked out my big hard cock along with my juicy and sweaty balls. I stroked myself slowly as Gabriel and Howard squeezed my tight butt cheeks a few times each.

"OHHHHH GOD, this feels awesome…" I moaned happily, the burning muscles in my arms mixed with the feeling of ecstasy somehow new.

In the full length mirror I watched myself jacking off. I had to admit that I was a pretty sight, hardy fucking har, har. I also watched as Gabriel and Howard stared in awe at my huge plump meat stick. Seeing the looks in their eyes spurred me on buds. What an ego trip this was let me tell you. A short while later I shot my pent-up load (my first of many that night) onto the mirror in front of us and we all watched as it dripped down to the floor.

"OH YEAH!!! YEAH!!!" I groaned my back slightly arched, looking real sexy in all my glory as I held my spewing cock aimed forward like it was a guided missile as I shot spew after spew of my good stuff.

Gabriel and Howard whooped it up, cheered me on, and slapped my butt as I shot another good sized mess of slop.

Moments later, after I had caught my breath I found myself roped tight at the wrists to the machine called "The Fly." (Howard had found some rope in a supply closet and suggested that I would look real cute and sexy all trussed up while I worked out on that machine.) On this machine a person sits straight up with their hands behind the mechanism that rotates the weights and works their chest. Howard was busy tying my feet as Gabriel told me that he wanted me to do five sets at sixty pounds each. I looked at him in incredulity.

"You fuckers, fun is fun, but you're going to kill me here!" I shouted at the two men.

"Nah, we're just helping you to get into real good shape!" Gabriel said, giving the back of my neck a light squeeze, stroking my hair. "Are his big ol' feet tied good and tight Howard?"

"They sure are," Howard replied and for fun snapped the elastic in my black sweat socks.

"Okay TJ my boy…start working!" Gabriel ordered.

I clenched my teeth and began rotating my arms on the machine. The first two sets weren't too difficult, but halfway through the third set I began to falter. Gabriel and Howard were there to help me along though buds. They rapped my hard on the legs with their damned leather belts a few times.

"OWWWWWWW!!!" I roared. "You fuckers!!"

When I was done with the fourth set I told them that I could not possibly do a fifth and pleaded with them to untie me from the machine. In response to my pleadings they belted my thighs <u>hard</u> until I forced myself to begin the fifth set.

"AAARRGHHHH!!!!" I screamed as I sweated and grunted through the fifth and final set.

When I was done I hung my head down and panted for breath. My thighs were a mess of red marks and stripes from their damned designer belts.

Once I had caught my breath Gabriel said, "Time for the next machine" and he and Howard untied me from the "Fly" machine. Holding me by my arms they walked me over to the shoulder press machine. They sat me down on it and Gabriel set the weight at eighty pounds.

"Ok TJ, five sets, starting now," Gabriel ordered.

I gripped the handles and began the shoulder exercises. I panted, grunted and swore like a madman through the sets, sweating profusely, really beginning to stink, seeing as I didn't get much of a break between the "Fly" machine and the shoulder press one I was now working on. When I completed my fifth set I instantly and without any prodding from my two captors grabbed my cock and began stroking it. I shuddered on the shoulder press machine and shot my damned load again, all over the rubber floor in front of me.

"OH YEAH, oh fuck yeah!!" I moaned loudly and in a real man's passion and pain.

Gabriel and Howard didn't know that my shoulders were pretty strong and that was why I had breezed through that exercise.

"Good going TJ ol' boy," Gabriel said, taking me by my arm.

He and Howard pulled me to my feet and brought me hastily over to the "chest press" machine. Somehow I got the feeling they didn't want me relaxing all that much in between working out. My cock hung comically out of my shorts as I was hustled along, it dripping remnants of my sticky juices on the gym floor.

"Let's tie this stack of muscles the fuck up again!" Howard said as they sat me on the seat of the "chest press" machine.

Gabriel dashed off to get the rope from where they had left it by the "Fly" machine. Howard twisted his fingers in my hair and I looked up at him.

"Fuckin' hot guy you are..." he whispered lustfully. "Going to tie you up again..."

"Somehow I get the feeling that you're really enjoying this man..." I replied.

As Gabriel tied rope around my waist, pinning me to the machine Howard did his dirty work winding rope around and around my feet, binding them tightly together. I noticed Howard looking hungrily at my dangling meat stick as it hung out of my shorts. He leaned forward, gave my cock two quick sucks, (which I should mention garnered a couple of good loud gasps of pleasure out of me) finished tying my feet, snapped the elastic in my black sweat socks again (god, that guy Howard really loved my feet let me tell you) and stood up. I gripped the handles of the machine, prepared to begin the workout.

"Okay TJ, lets get started," Gabriel said, setting the weight at one hundred pounds. "Five sets..."

When I completed the first two sets I hung my head down, sweating and shaking like crazy by then.

"Pl-please guys...n-no more..." I pleaded again. "I-I'm so...I'm so tired..."

Quickly, they reeled back and whacked their leather belts against my thighs, legs and arms.

"AAAARRRGGGGGHHHH!!!" I screamed at the onslaughts of varieties of pain.

"Work that chest TJ!!" Gabriel yelled at me. "You still have three more sets to go!"

Angrily, I clenched my teeth, grabbed the handles of the

machine tightly, and began my third set, screaming like a banshee, grunting like a soldier all the way through it. The fourth and fifth sets went the same way. I cursed and swore like an overly horned up marine as I finished the fifth set. My arms and chest aching I let go of the machine handles and looked up at the two grinning men.

"I don't know whether to hate you guys or to thank you for all of this!!" I said breathlessly.

Gabriel smiled fiendishly and pointed at my dangling flaccid cock…

"Bastards…" I whispered.

A short while later I was standing with my hands tied securely behind me and the slack of the rope extended down and tied off to a fifty pound weight on the floor. My feet were tied together as well. I was totally and fucking immobilized. Gabriel and Howard had had a grand old time stripping me of my sweat soaked tee shirt and shorts, looks of sheer and unadulterated ecstasy on their good-looking faces at the sight of my now bared huge muscular chest, my rock hard pecs and big round fleshy nipples. My two captors were now kneeling at my sides taking turns sucking the fuck out of my cock (which was now sticking out of my white briefs) and even licking my sweaty hairy balls real hard. They caressed my well-toned and shapely thighs and tree-trunk like legs at the same time, toying with my smelly socks. I squirmed in the bondage as my two handsome captors sucked me off, forcing me toward a third jazz shot.

"UUUNNNNN…" I moaned, my head thrown slightly back, my long salt and pepper colored hair hanging all sweaty behind my neck. "Bastards, milking me like I was a cow…milking me like crazy…draining my big balls…that's what you're doing!! AAAAARRRGHHHH!!! Easy with those damned balls of mine huh?"

"That's right TJ ol' boy," Gabriel said, looking up at me while Howard sucked the bejesus out of my aching muscle pipe. "We are going to siphon you till you can't stand it and then make you shoot even more creamy jazz for us! By the time this is over you 'll be totally fucking exhausted so you best keep cooking up batches of this good stuff buddy boy."

"AAARRRRRR!!!!" I screamed as I suddenly shot my load.

When I was done the two men untied me. I was sweating miserably, dizzy, God, my head was spinning. The two men hoisted me off the floor by my arms and legs, cradling me between themselves.

"Okay TJ, time for the lat pull-down machine," Gabriel said as they did me the honor of carrying me to the next machine.

"N-no more workouts…" I whimpered. "P-please…"

They set me down on the seat of the lat pull-down machine.

"Jeez, thanks for the lift," I mumbled sarcastically.

"No more workout?" Gabriel asked me. "TJ, we're just getting started on you big guy."

He slapped my naked and sweaty back hard with his open palm as Howard squeezed one of my pecs real hard, inflicting pain as he palmed it hard. I grimaced in pain at the sting of the slap on my back as it echoed through the gym.

"Now, its time to work on your back TJ," Gabriel said, setting the weight at ninety gruesome pounds. "Five sets begin!"

I stood up halfway and grabbed the bar, sitting back down again. I began the exercise. My back, like my shoulders is pretty strong and very well developed so I made it through all five sets without being belted. I saw the way my two captors were looking at my poor cock so to put on a bit of a show for them and to have some non-torturous workout time I grabbed my now really aching cock and began stroking it, HARD. It really took quite a while but I finally shot a very small load into my hand, grunting and moaning in tortured pleasure. Gabriel and Howard cheered me on, slapped my back hard, called me a hunky twenty-four hour beat off machine, and then yanked me roughly to my feet by my tired arms.

"You need water TJ," Gabriel said, noting how sweaty my entire body was at that point. "And maybe a protein drink as well... Howard, would you please go down to the main floor to the protein bar and mix our personal trainer here a good hearty protein drink?"

"Coming up," Howard said as he and Gabriel winked at each other in a conspiratorial fashion.

Howard sprinted off toward the stairs and Gabriel walked me to the water fountain. I gulped down mouthfuls of the icy cold water. Delicious... Howard returned a short while later with a lime flavored twenty ounce protein drink for me. I gulped that down as well, followed by more mouthfuls of water from the water fountain. When I was properly hydrated and feeling somewhat refreshed I was soon lying stretched out on an abdominal machine. My hands were crossed behind my back and tied at the wrists, my legs were stretched out in front of me, and I was doing stomach crunches. Gabriel knelt at the end of the bench I was on, slipped my sneakers off my feet and he and Howard were then kneeling at my feet and licking them, or, to be more precise, licking my stinking socked feet. (The perverts...) I was able to smell just how bad and raunchy my socked feet smelled and those two fuckers were licking them like they had been dipped in honey. I had been told by Gabriel to keep crunching my stomach until I was told to stop. Not being in a position to argue I did as I was told and watched as the two yuppies slobbered greedily over my feet.

"Man, his feet sure do fucking stink," Howard chuckled. "*Whew...*"

"Figures, the way we're working him," Gabriel replied. "When we're all done we'll keep his smelly socks as a souvenir of all this."

"Fuckers..." I grunted. "First you kidnap me...then you steal my damned socks..."

They laughed. When I had rolled my damned socks on that morning I had no fucking idea that they would become the property of two sadistic yuppies. I was up to fifty crunches and starting to grunt in pain. I was also feeling kind of hard, sore and sleazy in the cock as well. I figured that the sight of the two handsome and maniacal yuppies licking my socked feet was getting me hard all over again. I figured I would have no problem shooting another load...when the time came. What I didn't know at that moment as I stomach crunched was actually just how easy I would find it to shoot another load so soon...seeing as my protein drink had been spiked. My cock grew tingly as I crunched. God, I had never shot my load so many times in such a short stretch...even when I was a teenager... At one hundred crunches I begged Gabriel and Howard to allow me to stop but now, *now,* they were jacking themselves off as they continued licking and slobbering all over my feet...I was told to keep crunching while they jacked off. I supposed that all the misery they had heaped on me had really gotten their cock's churning, seeing as they were both close to spewing their loads. Gabriel shot his load first, discharging his mess all over my saliva and sweat soaked stinking socks followed a few short seconds later by Howard. The two men roared, grunted, and swore in real passion as they ejected their hefty loads all over my feet. I could feel their warm juices as they sluiced even through my thick black sweat socks. When they were done they slowly licked their cum off my feet. My cock was feeling sleazier yet, which was mystifying to me, seeing as I had shot how many loads myself at that point? I began to wonder what the fuck was going on with my manhood. I was up to one hundred and fifty crunches, buds, I was sweating and my stomach area was hurting like the devil.

"G-guys, please…" I begged.

Finally, Gabriel told me to stop crunching but to stay stretched out on the machine. I did as I was told and watched with my cock stiffening more yet as they licked the remaining remnants of their cum from my socks…

It was now twelve thirty at night. After I had finished my crunches Gabriel and Howard didn't make me jack off. It seemed they wanted to frustrate me a while this time around. With that in mind I knew that the protein drink that they had given me had been spiked somehow. I surmised that I had been tricked into scoffing down some kind of potent aphrodisiac. It was the only explanation as to why my exhausted cock would be standing at attention after the times I had already shot my load mixed with the fact that I was physically exhausted from all the workouts I was being forced murderously through. No, instead of being made to jack off again I was given a fifteen minute break from the brutal workout the two sadistic yuppies were putting me through. I drank long gulps of water, stretched my aching limbs, and lay down on the bench of the free weight chess press machine. I closed my eyes as Gabriel and Howard leaned over me and each of them sucked one of my nipples.

"Oh yeah, work on my man sized nipples you two..." I groaned. "OOOOOO yeah, lick those fucking tits of mine!!"

As they slurped and sucked my nipples with true gusto my cock was as hard and unbending as concrete. I gripped the sides of the bench I was lying on as Howard's hand closed around my aching cock as he continued sucking my nipple that he had in his mouth. Gabriel stood up and yanked my hands above me to the bar where the weights behind me were neatly stacked.

"WHA..." I said in surprise.

"Relax TJ ol' boy," Gabriel said. "I just feel like tying you the fuck up again!"

As Gabriel meanly wound the rope around my wrists and to the weight bar my cock was pounding with a life all it's own in Howard's hand.

"GOD almighty, you two are driving me batty!!!" I exclaimed.

Gabriel quickly resumed sucking my nipple that he had momentarily abandoned and Howard began stroking my hardness. The combination of it all, being tied up again, having my nipples tortured and pleasured at the same time, being stripped to my damned socks and under shorts, and being stroked to a another fucking jazz shot was definitely driving me utterly insane. I sweated and panted like crazy and creamed in Howard's hand. My sweaty testicles rocked up and down against the bench as I drained them yet again that night.

"OH GOD yeah!!!" I roared as I ejected my mess. "FUCKING YEAH!!!"

Howard licked the small amount of cum off his hand and

then lifted my socked feet onto the bench I was lying on. He quickly roped my feet together at the ankles, sniffing and snuffling at my smelly socks at the same time.

"Let's jack off again Gabriel," Howard piped up anxiously. "I'm hornier than a bitch in heat on a summer night. This fucking guy makes my nuts churn."

Again the two men took position at my feet and started jacking themselves off, prepared to shoot their loads again all over my damned feet. They stroked their cocks like crazy, they stroked each other's cocks and back again at themselves…and I watched in tied up ecstasy as they shot and shot their second loads each…all over my stinking feet.

"OH yeah!!!" they grunted as I had just minutes ago. "FUCKING A!!!"

Amazingly, my cock grew semi hard again as I watched the two yuppies lick their cum off my socks. I supposed that whatever aphrodisiac they had fed me was still working its magical charms on my manhood. I discovered that night that I indeed got off on watching guys lick my socked feet. I vowed that from then on I would make sure to search out guys who got off on licking another guy's feet. When they were done Gabriel untied my hands from the weight bar and slung me up over his broad shoulders, his hand resting somewhat tenderly on my butt.

"Let's get him working again," Gabriel said, running the palm of his hand over my butt cheeks. "I don't want our boy resting too much."

"You fuckers…" I whispered miserably as Gabriel carried me over his shoulder like I was a sack of dirty laundry to the triceps machine.

With my sneakers back on my feet I stood with my hands on the bar of the triceps machine. Gabriel set the weight at eighty pounds.

"Okay TJ, here's the deal with this machine..." Gabriel said as Howard kneeled in front of me and gobbled my semi erection into his mouth.

"UUUNNNNNNNN!!!" I moaned breathlessly as Howard held my meat snugly in his craw.

"There's no limit on the amount of reps you'll do on this machine," Gabriel explained and squeezed one of my nipples, getting another breathless moan out of me. "As you workout Howard will suck your cock. Isn't that great TJ? I mean, how many guys out there can say that they've had their pride and joy sucked while they worked out?"

"H-how many guys out there can say that their damned pride and joy was feeling the way mine is right now while they worked out?" I gasped as Howard swirled his tongue teasingly over my cock in his mouth.

"Good point TJ," Gabriel said agreeably and chuckled. "You will stop the exercise after you've cum. And that should take you a while, seeing as, just as you've pointed out, that cock of yours has to be totally sore and spent by now. But then, with the drink we gave you, you shouldn't really have a problem. I suppose we'll find out eh?"

"*Y-you spiked my protein drink?*" I asked him miserably as I gripped the triceps handle weight bar. "That's a fucked up thing to do a guy who's a health nut buddy!"

"You noticed eh?" Gabriel asked, pointing down at my cock in Howard's mouth.

Howard looked up joyously as he held my meat in his warm mouth.

Gabriel then tied a white cloth over my eyes, blindfolding me.

"Shit man…" I whispered. "I didn't think you would blindfold me too…"

"Start the exercise!" Gabriel shouted.

When I began the exercise, tugging the triceps bar down and then back up Howard began sucking my manhood in earnest.

"UUUHHHHFFF!!!" I bellowed in a mixture of definite pleasure and pain.

After about twenty reps my arms were aching and my cock was raging and hard in Howard's mouth. He deep throated me a few times, teased my piss slit with his tongue and sucked me like a madman but honestly, I was nowhere near to cumming. I felt his fingers toying with my balls. Man, if I was able to have seen that I would have cum already. I love watching my big kiwi-sized nuts played with, almost as much as I love watching my feet get a good tongue bath. They had figured by then that I got off on watching, that was when I knew why Gabriel had blindfolded me. They had figured out that I got off on watching all the kinky stuff they were heaping on me, their conquered muscle headed personal trainer. They were onto me. Inwardly they knew that it was actually me controlling this entire scene. At thirty reps I was in horrible and searing pain. I begged for it to be over, even though I hadn't yet shot my load. When I paused during the exercise Gabriel got me moving by whacking me across the legs with his belt a few times.

"AAARRRGGHHH!!!" I screamed loudly.

Finally, *of God finally,* after forty reps and with my triceps literally burning with fatigue I shot a small squirt of a load into Howard's mouth.

"AAAAYYYRRRRR!!!" I roared as I came in small spurts. "WH-what a feeling, GAWD!!"

I let go of the exercise bar, Gabriel removed my blindfold, and I stood there catching my breath, my head hanging down, almost crying to say it plainly.

"P-please...no more...no more..." I begged.

Gabriel stood in front of me and kissed me tenderly on the lips. It was the kindest and most tender gesture he had bestowed on me since he and Howard had captured me.

"You did well TJ," Gabriel said, holding my face in his hands. "You sure as shit can take it. Come on, let's go take a shower."

I fell against him and was grateful as he lifted me over his shoulders. He carried me down to the shower room, followed by Howard. In the shower I let the warm water soothe my aching and pumped up body as I lathered soap all over myself. When I emerged from the shower (feeling somewhat better) and walked naked into the locker room with a towel draped over my neck I found Gabriel and Howard sitting on the bench where I had first met them...all those hours ago now. They were each holding one of my black sweat socks in their hands, the souvenirs of their conquest. My underpants, tee shirt, and sneakers were all on the floor next to them.

"Feelin' good TJ?" Gabriel asked me.

"Better," I said. "You two really worked me over hard.

The two men smiled at each other.

"Well you know TJ ol' TJ, there's still the cardio vascular area," Gabriel mused. "We didn't get near the exercise bikes, the treadmills, the stair masters..."

"No, no...you wouldn't..." I whispered in terror.

Ten minutes later, dressed only in my damned under shorts, I sat tied to the seat of an exercise bike and pedaled furiously as Gabriel and Howard whacked and thrashed my ass cheeks over and over with their leather belts. It turned out to be a long night at the gym that night...

After what I guessed to be an hour or so Officer Ryder stopped the car and the trunk was opened. I was a sweating and shaking mess. More to the point I was a shaking and terror-stricken mess. In seconds I was on my knees on a deserted road. Alex and Ronald stood over me sipping bottles of cool mineral water as I alternately sucked their cocks, which were hanging out of the fly openings in their jeans. Ryder stood a few feet away, leaning on his patrol cruiser, him also sipping a bottle of mineral water, watching the spectacle in front of him. I could feel him looking at me as he seemed to be assessing me as I sucked his buddies' cocks. My hands were of course still cuffed behind me (as they would remain for a long time) and now I was blindfolded...with a long white strip of my gym uniform tee shirt, which the two men had ripped off me and to shreds after hauling me roughly from the car trunk. It was at Ryder's orders that they had torn my tee shirt off me, exposing my well-muscled body, and proceeded to use a strip of the torn tee shirt to blindfold me with.

"OOOHHRRRRR man feels so fucking good..." Alex

crooned heartily, stroking my long hair as I sucked his semi hard cock, poking my tongue into his dick slit.

"Yeah, get back over here you scumbag…" Ronald demanded and stuffed his throbbing cock into my mouth after Alex had slid his out. "AHHHHH yeah, suck my cock you bastard…"

"You two are enjoying that over there eh?" I heard Ryder ask from where he was standing.

"Oh yeah man, fucking guy can sure suck a cock…" Ronald said breathlessly, his fingers entwined in my hair as he raped my mouth.

"Well guys, this is just the beginning of a great fucking day…" Ryder said. "With what I have planned for this poor slob you two will be kissing my boots in thanks by day's end…"

"Okay asshole, back to chowing on my dick now," Alex said sternly and Ronald pulled his cock out of my mouth.

Alex slid his manhood back into my mouth and I sucked him like crazy as he face fucked the very hell out of me.

"Take it easy Alex, you'll get your cock sucked all you want by that fucking guy…" Officer Ryder said jovially. "No need to be so demanding and greedy about it. He's got no choice in all of this and he knows it, the handsome fuck."

"OHHHHRRR man Ryder, but it feels so warm and toasty in this mouth of his…" Alex swooned. "Could keep my meat pole in there all day…"

"Well, we don't have all day to be here on this road man…" Ryder said. "After you two horned up fucks make him gulp down your jazz make him drink your piss…if you need to piss that is… Remember, pissing on the road out here is against the law."

"Don't worry about that Ryder," Ronald responded, rubbing the tip of his manhood against my face as I sucked Alex. "I'll fucking force myself to piss if I have to…come on guy, back to sucking my cock now…"

Before I sucked Ronald's cock back into my mouth after Alex had slid his out I piped up angrily at Ryder, saying, "Yeah, pissing on the road out here is illegal, but I suppose kidnapping a poor guy is totally on the up and up huh???" To shut me up Ronald fed me his cock and I obligingly sucked him…

After about fifteen minutes or so of really sucking the fuck out of the two cop's cocks they both shot their loads…one behind the other. I was forced to guzzle down their slop (fuck, they seemed to cum and cum and cum) and then they did just as Ryder had suggested, namely they made me drink their rancid and vile tasting piss.

"OHHHHRRR man, that was so fucking good…" Alex crooned and I heard the sound of his zipper being pulled up.

I knelt there with what had to be the worst tasting and scented mouth in creation…

"Glad you two enjoyed that, but there's plenty more where that came from…" Ryder said. "Damn, I have to piss too now… fuckin' mineral water goes right the fuck through me. Hey, get the fuck over here Mr. John, good name for you at the moment!! Walk on your damned knees over to me so I can piss in that hole in your face."

I took a deep anguished sounding breath, hunched my shoulders back miserably, and slowly made my way over to the man who had captured me, on my damned knees. The hard road scraped up my knees but Ryder didn't seem all that overly concerned.

"C'mon you flunky, move it!!" Ryder demanded. "I really have to piss, and I don't want to piss on the ground. Like I said, that's against the law out here..."

When I was kneeling in front of him I leaned my head back, dropped my mouth open, and drank Ryder's piss as he emptied his bladder into me. My poor knees felt awful as I scoffed down the cop's piss.

"AHHHH yeah, much better..." Ryder exclaimed sadistically as I gulped down his rancid tasting piss...not losing a single drop of it.

When he was done I was back on my feet, standing there shirtless, still cuffed and blindfolded. My knees felt all scraped up and raw and I stood there miserably as the men stole hard squeezes of my tits, really mashing and pinching the fuck out of them. They slapped my pecs hard, yanked out a few of my chest hairs, (that really got a good loud moan of anguish out of me) and slapped my stomach a few good hard ones also. I stood there grunting and groaning as the three men, cops, really worked on me. My cock throbbed long and hard in my shorts...in total fear...totally betraying me... This was not like being trapped at the gym with Gabriel and Howard, this was really horrifying...I had been abducted by three psycho cops and had no idea if I would survive the ordeal this time around.

"Okay you two load that stack of shit back into the trunk of my patrol car and we'll get moving again," Ryder said to his two buddies as they pawed me. "There'll be plenty of time to torture those nips of his very soon. The way I see it we should be at my farm within twenty minutes..."

Alex and Ronald hoisted me back into the trunk of Ryder's patrol car and slammed the lid shut. As the car started again I licked my piss and cum tasting lips, total fear consuming me. My tears flowed again behind my blindfold. As the car moved along the highway I again thought back to the fateful night at the gym with Gabriel and Howard…to the moment after they had tied me to the exercise bike and were rapping my poor ass cheeks with their leather belts as I pedaled…and pedaled…and pedaled…

Pedaling…pedaling…I was pedaling furiously with my teeth clenched, on the damned exercise bike that Gabriel and Howard had tied me to. I was sweating profusely (dripping with sweat from head to toe by then to be exact) as they pummeled my ass cheeks with their leather belts. I screamed out in pain each time they would thrash my poor backside. I had been on that bike and pedaling for close to an hour at that point…and by all points the two yuppies were not about to let me off it any time soon. Fuck it all, they were having too much fun watching me cook and sweat my guts out. Howard put a bottle of mineral water to my lips every few minutes to make sure I would not dehydrate. I sipped it vigorously, loving the taste of the cool water as it slid down my throat. I pedaled more and more…and they thrashed my ass cheeks more and more… As I pedaled like a madman I thought about the moment they had captured me again in the locker room…right after I had finished showering after the brutal workout they had already forced me through…thinking that I was finally going home for the night. Turned out that was not their plan for me at all. I found the two men sitting where I had first encountered them. They were each holding one of my black and stinking sweat socks…the souvenirs of their conquest of me…the big and burly gym instructor. They jokingly told me how we had not even looked at the cardio vascular machines. When I realized they were serious about working me over some more I gulped…and gulped hard buds… Gabriel picked up my sweaty sopped and smelly under shorts, sniffed them vigorously, and tossed them over to me. With trembling hands I pulled them on, wondering when this long night would be over. The two men dropped my souvenir socks on the floor by their lockers, took me roughly by my aching and pumped up arms, and amid my pleading (what they really wanted to hear) for no more they walked me to the elevator that would take us again back up to the gym. In the elevator they yanked my arms meanly behind me and chowed down on my nipples, getting some real loud grunts and groans out of me. Besides all pumped up and aching from the workout they had put me through I was also very sensitized and sexy feeling from all the times I had been made to shoot my load. As they feasted on my nipples my cock became all tingly in my sweat matted briefs...what a feeling buds...

"Mmm, you smell real fresh and soapy TJ ol' boy..." Howard said and resumed sucking my nipple.

"Yeah, but very soon he'll smell real foul and manly again..." Gabriel said as the elevator door slid open.

They hustled me over to an exercise bike, hoisted me up onto the seat and roped my wrists to the handlebars. They tied me down to the seat by winding rope over and over my muscular thighs and under and over the seat itself. It looked like I was wearing a pair of shorts made out of rope. They then set the bike's tension level at six, and ordered me to get busy pedaling. With no choice but to obey I did as I was told...having my butt whacked hard with their leather belts as I pedaled like my life depended on it...

And so, close to an hour later I was still pedaling...and still having my butt belted...

"G-guys please..." I panted. "Wh-when are you going to let me off this thing? My legs are burning!"

"Just keep pedaling TJ," Gabriel said and rapped my butt

hard with his belt.

"YOWWWWWW!!!" I screeched.

"A gym instructor such as yourself should be able to endure this and lots more..." Gabriel teased me, raised his belt and swatted my ass again.

"YOWWWWWW!!!" I screeched again.

Finally, after an hour and ten minutes Gabriel ordered me to stop pedaling. I did, gratefully. The two yuppies untied me and helped me off the bike to my bare feet. I stood between them catching my breath as they ran their hands over my sweaty and stinking body.

"Oh yeah TJ," Gabriel said as he squeezed one of my nipples and twisted it like it was a bottle cap. "Lookin' good, working fucking hard..."

"Real fucking hard..." Howard said and slapped my butt.

"*Fuckers...*" I whispered.

Minutes later they had wound some rope lightly around my neck and then tied my wrists together behind my neck with the slack of the rope, giving them easy access to my rancid smelling bushy armpits. I stood as still as possible as the two sleazy perverts slathered their tongues all over me, lapping up and eating the sweat off me, driving me into a new sexual frenzy. As they licked and sucked my smelly armpits they squeezed and flicked my sore nipples with their fingers and thumbs.

"OHHHRRRRR you goddamned guys are driving me crazy..." I croaked breathlessly.

They squatted at my sides and licked my sweat from my under shorts, running and strumming their tongues over them, caressing my thighs at the same time. Exhausted as I was I was swooning in total and sheer ecstasy…and I wondered when it would be time to jack off again…and shoot what would feel like the umpteenth load. I moaned and groaned in the state of ecstasy that my two captors had forced me to, over the top actually. They pulled my under shorts down in the back and ran their tongues over my red ass cheeks.

"OHHHHH YEAH…" I crooned.

My cock was now super hard in my under shorts but the two men stopped licking my butt and stood up at my sides.

"Okay TJ ol' boy, time for the stair master now…" Gabriel said and slapped my butt real hard.

"OWWWWWWW!!! *Shit…*" I whispered.

They untied my wrists and walked me over to one of the stair master machines. In moments I was standing on the machine and climbing the imaginary flights of stairs…blindfolded, and with my damned under shorts still yanked down in the back, talk about totally fucking mortifying! Gabriel and Howard stood behind me, reaching up and rapping my ass cheeks with their belts, reddening them even more.

"AAARRHHHHHH!!!" I roared like a trapped lion as they rapped my butt cheeks harder and harder with each blow.

"He really can take it eh Gabriel?" Howard asked his sadistic buddy.

"He sure as shit can Howard…" Gabriel replied and whacked my butt again and again with his belt. "He sure as all shit can."

Being blindfolded and being repeatedly whacked with their belts made it seem as though I really was climbing endless flights of stairs. I again began sweating my guts out. Howard reached up and handed me the bottle of mineral water a few times in between my climbing and I chugged it down greedily.

"How many flights are we going to make him do?" I heard Howard ask Gabriel.

"I don't know yet," Gabriel replied. "Listen, run down to the locker room and get his sneakers and socks. I want to put him on a treadmill next and I don't want him doing that barefooted."

"Sure, but those socks are ours now..." Howard said.

"Yeah, and after he's worn them and sweated in them a while more they'll be even more ripe," Gabriel said to Howard. "Go get them buddy..."

I heard Howard walk away and Gabriel continued whacking my exposed butt cheeks with his leather belt.

"AAAARHHHHHHH!!!" I cried out.

"Climb faster TJ," Gabriel demanded. "You're going to do some miles on a treadmill after this!!"

He whacked my poor butt again.

"AAAARRRRRR!!!" I roared in awful pain. "L-listen to me already man!! Th-this is a horrendous way to make a guy work-out! I'm aching, I-I am so fucking blasted and tired..."

"Then you'll sleep well when you're home later..." Gabriel

teased me and whacked my butt again...and again...and again...

I climbed the stair master, one foot over the other, sweat pouring off me everywhere...

A short while later Howard returned with my sneakers and stinking socks. The two men forced me to climb nearly one hundred flights of stairs and then I was ordered to stop. The machine stopped and I sank to the floor, still standing on the steps of the stair master. My two captors helped me off the machine and Gabriel took my blindfold off for me. He and Howard steadied me by my arms between them as I stood there gasping, panting uncontrollably, practically crying, trying to catch my breath.

"G-guys please..." I begged.

They squeezed my nipples and kissed me on the trembling lips a few times each. When Gabriel wrapped his arms around me and kissed me hard on the lips I felt Howard's tongue licking my searing red butt cheeks, soothing them a bit for me.

"Fucking hot guy you are TJ..." Gabriel whispered in my ear, his fingers tangled in my sopping wet hair.

When my cock was hard again in my under shorts they stopped kissing me and licking my damned sexy ass. It seemed that for round two of my workout they were not letting my shoot my load as much as I had done during the first round. Instead I was being sexually frustrated, which in a way was just as well. Fucking fucks, I was too tired even to crank my crank buds. The two yuppies then ordered me to get my sneakers and socks on and to get my ass on one of the treadmills. Once again I did as I was told and very soon I was running in place on a fast moving treadmill, the sounds of my feet pounding on the conveyer as I ran, ran, running for my life it seemed. Gabriel and Howard did not whack my exposed butt cheeks this time; instead they sat on the floor on the sides of the machine I was on, chatting.

"How much more do you want to put him through?" Howard asked Gabriel.

"I really haven't decided just yet," Gabriel replied, looking around the gym. "I still want him to use the legs and thighs machines. We'll put him on the prone leg curl machine next. In the position he'll be in on there, all bent over with his sexy ass in the air we can really pulverize the fuck out of his butt with our belts. FUCK, he won't sit comfortably for a week, ha!"

"Yeah, great fucking idea, and we can tie him to that machine too!!" Howard said anxiously.

Fucking Howard, he sure had a definite love for tying me the fuck up let me tell you. The way they were talking about me and talking about what they were going to do to me as if I wasn't even there was extremely angering. I ran faster on the treadmill, clenched my teeth, and pounded my feet hard against the moving floor. When I had run a total of eight miles and was dripping with sweat again the two men stood up on the sides of the machine, leering at me.

"Man, he looks really beat to shit..." Howard said, sounding almost sympathetic.

"Yeah, he does," Gabriel agreed. "Okay TJ ol' boy, stop running..."

I pressed the "stop" button on the treadmill console and the conveyer under my feet stopped. I grabbed the bars on the sides of the machine, hung my head down, and breathed heavily...

"Let's give him a break before we put him on the next machine," Gabriel said.

I looked at him angrily. Together the two men helped me off the machine and Gabriel again slung me up and over his shoulders. He carried me toward the massage room, followed by Howard.

"WH-what now???" I asked breathlessly as I was lugged along like a sack of potatoes. "What the fuck now?"

In the massage room Gabriel laid me down on my stomach on the towel covered table and splayed my legs apart, dangling them real sexily off the sides of said table.

"Oh man Gabriel, I know just what the fuck you have in mind for our boy now..." Howard said, looking at my exposed pink and raunchy bunghole. "Oh fuck what a sweet looking opening he has..."

The two sadist yuppies squatted behind me and took turns licking, sucking and eating the fuck out of my stinking and most private crevice. I gripped the sides of the table as goose bumps broke out and took like all over my musculature.

"OHHHHHRRRR yeah, yeah, fucking A you two!!" I crooned as they worked my anal cavity like two bitches in heat. "FUCKING totally awesome you guys, motherfuckin' A!!"

I raised my upper body upwards off the table and looked behind me as they ate my hole and drove me wild with a man's passion, working and working my stinking bunghole. It looked at one point as if they were actually fighting over it, each of them aching and vying to plunge their tongue into it.

"OHHHHH fuck..." I whispered and lay back down.

After a long while they stopped eating my hole and began taking turns prodding it with their fingers, stretching it, torturing it erotically, and in the whole of what they were doing, out rightly driving me practically insane with delight.

"Okay, he's wet as a duck's bottom back here…"Gabriel said. "Fucking hot TJ is ready…"

"Let's oil him up a bit," Howard suggested, grabbing a bottle of massage oil from a shelf.

Smiling, the two men dripped massage oil deep into my asshole and worked it in liberally with their fingers, sticking two and three fingers at a time deep into my velvety warmness back there.

"OHHHRRRRR yeah!!" I roared and began rocking back and forth atop the table, rubbing my hard cock against the table-top. "Want to shoot my load so bad…"

After my hole was lubed like it never had been before the two men stopped oiling it and dropped their shorts. Both of their cocks were hard as concrete and throbbing, ready to plow my moist and ready hole. Gabriel went first. The horny fucker climbed up on the table behind me and slowly and almost lovingly slid his pole into my hole.

"OHHHHHHHRRRR yeah fuck me you yuppie bastard!!" I wailed in sheer ecstasy. "Fuck that sopped wet hole of mine!!"

Gabriel plunged his thick cock all the way inside my hole and began thrusting in and out of me like crazy, driving me wild as he piled drove me and made my head spin.

"Oh yeah, what a tight hole you have TJ ol' boy!!" Gabriel grunted as he fucked me harder and harder. "Tight fucking hole…"

The yuppie bastard that he was, Gabriel shot his load into my hole, flooding me good and deep. It felt so HOT as he sluiced inside me. When he was done he slid his cock slowly out of my hole, shuddering as he went and hopped down off the table. Howard wasted no time, quickly taking Gabriel's place behind me up on the table.

"Oh yeah, your turn..." I groaned at Howard as he slid his hardness inside me next.

As Howard fucked me it felt like my hole was literally eating his cock, sucking and pulling it in as far as humanly possible.

"Fuck him good..." Gabriel said, standing at the side of the table.

Howard thrust deep and plowed my hole and I rocked faster and faster on the table, getting ready to shoot my load. When Howard shot his load he roared like an animal and at the same damned time I shot my load...right into my pulled down under shorts. A few minutes passed as the two men and I caught our breath. I sat up on the table and looked at them in disbelief.

"Oh man, you two are unfuckingbelievable..." I said to them in passion.

They stepped over to me and tongued one of my nipples each, sending chills through me. I leaned my head back and swooned. Every part of me was sensitive to the touch at the moment and the way they were tonguing my nipples was making me crazy... But then, without a word, they hoisted me off the table and carried me out of the massage room and over to the prone leg curl machine... It seemed fun time was over...for the moment...

They laid me on the prone leg curl machine bent over on

my stomach with my hands on the handles of the device in front of me. They then positioned my socked ankles under the bar that would lift the weights. Gabriel roped my wrists tightly to the handles of the machine as Howard slowly and methodically tied my feet together. The sleazy fucker was sniffing my damned socks as he tied my feet. I got to say it again man, that Howard sure had a thing for tying me up *and* for my smelly feet and socks. Gabriel set the weight at sixty five pounds. My under shorts were still pulled down in the back…I didn't need three guesses to know what that meant.

"Okay TJ, five sets…" Gabriel said as he and Howard stood behind me. "Begin!!"

I lifted the weight with my tied ankles and curled it back toward my thighs. As I let the weight down my two captors each gave my upturned ass cheeks a quick hard whack with their belts.

"OWWWWW!!!" I yelled and continued working out.

I worked as quickly as possible. The quicker I finished all five sets the quicker they would stop belting my poor behind.

"Damn Gabriel, look at how his ass cheeks jiggle as belt em'," Howard laughed and rapped me hard.

"OWWWWWWW!!!" I roared.

"Yeah, just like a fucking bowl of Jell-O…" Gabriel agreed and gave my ass a good hard whack. "Fucking great piece of ass ol' TJ is…"

Later, when I was done with all five sets the two yuppies stopped belting me and untied my wrists and ankles. I stood up and thoroughly stretched my arms and legs. Gabriel handed me the bottle of mineral water and I gulped it down, finishing it off.

"Well TJ, I would say at this point that we are done working you over," Gabriel said and squeezed one of my nipples. "This time we mean it. You really were a good sport and a stand-up kind of guy about it all."

"Yeah man, like I said, you sure as shit can take it," Howard said.

I shook hands with both of them, a small smile (mostly of relief) on my lips.

"I don't know if I should say thanks or what..." I said to them. "Never been through a workout quite like this one before in my entire life..."

"Maybe you should say lets do it again some time," Gabriel suggested.

We all laughed and I said I didn't think so, adding how being worked over once in the way they had done to me was more than enough to last a guy a while. We all walked down to the locker room, Gabriel and Howard to get dressed, and me to take another much needed shower before finally heading home... Down in the locker room Gabriel and Howard got dressed, putting on their business suits. I have to say here that they looked mighty spiffy and real handsome all done up in their office attire. Somehow, seeing them fully clothed in their suits, their shirts and ties, spit polished shoes, it made me proud of myself for having endured what these two men had put me through. I took off my sneakers and socks and handed one of my smelly socks to each of them.

"Here you go guys," I said, handing them my moist and rancid smelling black socks. "I would say that for sure you have earned these."

"Thanks TJ," Gabriel said, taking one of the prized socks from me. "But you know, I just had another thought…"

"WH-what thought is that?" I asked him nervously, wondering just what the hell he had in mind for me now.

The Next Morning…

The gym opens at six AM on weekdays and it was my buddies Jerry and Ralph's day to open up on the day after Gabriel and Howard had worked me over. When my buddies opened the front door the first thing they did was walk down to the locker rooms and turn on all the lights. It's usual procedure to open the gym from the bottom floor first and to work your way up to the top floor. Also, its usual procedure to check that there's hot water while down in the locker room area where the showers are as well. When Jerry and Ralph turned on the lights in the men's locker room they both let out a loud collective gasp at the sight before them. Gabriel and Howard had tied me to a concrete post in the center of the locker room. My muscular and tired arms were pulled around the sides of the post and rope was wound tightly around my upper well-toned body, under and over my pecs, really accenting my fleshy nipples, pinning me tightly to the post. My legs were pressed together and tied up at the thighs, the knees and the ankles to the post. I was totally immobilized and wearing just my white very soggy under shorts.

"Oh shit, TJ!!" Jerry yelled and rushed over to me, followed by Ralph. "Wh-what the fuck happened man??? Were you robbed or something??"

"Don't ask questions guys, please…" I seethed angrily. "Just untie me."

It was awful enough what Gabriel and Howard had done to me, but mortifying to say the least to leave me tied up in the locker room all night for two of my buddies to find in the morning.

"First tell us what happened," Ralph said, pushing Jerry's hand away from the knots in the ropes when he saw the bulge I was sporting in my under shorts.

So I told them. I told them how Gabriel and Howard had abducted me and of how they had worked me over by making me workout big fucking time in the gym. I told of how they had made me jack off numerous times to the point that my cock ached. I told of how I had been tricked into drinking a potent aphrodisiac mixed with my protein drink. Lastly, I told of how the two sadistic yuppies had fucked my ass like two plow machines, and how they had left with my socks as a souvenir.

"Damn TJ, they took your socks? Your smelly socks?" Ralph asked me comically. "They must have stunk to God's highest heaven man, those socks. I mean, I've been right next to you after a workout when you've taken those stinkers off your feet here in the locker room…and I gotta tell you buddy, the smell nearly killed me. *Phew…*"

Fuck, the guy was more amazed at the sleazy fact that my captors had taken my damned socks, rather than showing any concern for what I told him I had been forced through.

"Never mind how my socks are scented after a workout man…" I said desperately, practically pleading. "Please untie me you guys…I am fucking exhausted. Every part of me is aching…those fuckers…they left me tied up like this for hours…"

"Yeah, you sure do look tired," Ralph said. "And pumped… you look really, *really* pumped up… Say Jerry, are you thinking what I'm thinking?"

"I think I'm thinking what you're thinking Ralph, I fucking think so..."Jerry said with a fiendish look on his face.

Second later my two buddies were each sucking, bighting and tonguing my nipples, helping themselves to me like I was a goddamned buffet.

"OHHHHRRRR GAWD, here we go again..." I moaned miserably. "Hell, some buddies you two turned out to be!"

We arrived at Ryder's farm about twenty minutes later or so...I guess. The car stopped again and I was hauled roughly from the interior of the trunk. My blindfold had slid down to just above my nose, but I still kept my eyes squeezed shut...not wanting Ryder to see that I could see if I wanted to.

"Well, here we are asshole...home sweet fucking home for the day..." Ryder said, hooking a hand around my upper arm as I stood there on wobbly legs.

I heard Alex and Ronald slam the doors shut on the cars they had been driving and they walked over to us. Instantly their fingers were roaming on me, squeezing my man sized nipples and running their hands open palmed over my musculature.

"Some farm..." Alex said. "Looks like a bomb hit it."

"I had said I inherited a farm..."Ryder said to Alex, still holding my arm tight. "I didn't say what kind of shape it was in. But not to worry, my guy here will help in getting some things fixed up around here..."

The three men laughed and I grimaced miserably as

Ryder squeezed my arm tight.

"Let's get this blindfold off him now, I'm sure Mr. John wants to see the place after all..." Ryder said and pulled the blindfold off me.

I opened my eyes and let them adjust to the sunlight. I stood there shirtless and shaking in my sneakers and shorts as Alex and Ronald went on squeezing my nipples hard...taking in the sight of the very rundown looking farm. The barn looked like it hadn't been painted in years, the grounds were all overgrown with weeds, the tool shed looked like it was about to fall down, and the house, big as it was needed extensive work done on it. As Ryder had mentioned earlier it was completely surrounded by woods.

"Well Mr. John, it's not much of a farm, but you'll help to get it whipped into shape..."Ryder said, taking his hand off my arm and stroking my long hair in the back, squeezing the back of my neck at the same time. "Because if you don't get it whipped into shape I'll whip you into shape..."

As Ryder spoke and squeezed the back of my neck Alex and Ronald leaned down and they each greedily slurped one of my big nipples into their mouths.

"OHHHRRRR..." I gasped, flinging my head back a bit as the two cops feasted meanly on my tits.

"Really like those tits of his eh you two?" Ryder asked with a grin on his face. "Okay, seeing as you agreed to all this with me I'll let you suck and slurp on 'em for a few minutes but then I'm putting our boy here to work...*and I mean hard fucking work...*"

Ryder took his hand off the back of my neck and walked away from us toward the tool shed. As Ryder walked toward the shed I could not help but notice how fucking awesome and astounding his ass looked in his uniform pants. Two melons shaped globes, a real tight bubble butt if I ever saw one. The two other guys sucking my nipples only added to the excitement (and the fear) I was feeling at that moment.

"Shit you guys, what is this?" I whispered breathlessly, not wanting Ryder to hear me speaking without his permission. "Take a guy out to a rundown old farm and suck the fuck out of his big old man nips???"

"I don't know what Ryder has planned for you man, but for the moment you should really enjoy this while you can," Ronald said and instantly resumed sucking my nipple.

"OHHHHH yeah…feels great…" I panted.

"Yeah, because if I know Ryder you are in for one hell of a fucking time…" Alex added, tweaking my nipple which had been in his mouth as he spoke. "He has a definite sadistic streak in him…"

"You can say that again…" I replied miserably.

Alex slurped my nipple back into his mouth and the two men went on sucking my nips and running their hands over my body, stealing squeezes at the bulge in my shorts at the same time. With all the trouble I was in at the moment I stupidly realized I would not be at the LA gym for my first day on the job. I also wondered if they would make me pay for the shirt that Alex and Ronald had torn off me.

"OHHHRRRR SHIT, yeah, suck my nips you guys…" I panted.

The two men grabbed the sides of my gym shorts and

tugged on them hard, ripping them off me, revealing my white Calvin Klein briefs and the big plump bulge that was pressing against them in front...oozing pre cum through the white cotton material. When I looked up again I saw Officer Ryder coming back from the tool shed. He was carrying an old looking, rusty pitchfork. As he got closer I saw that the pitchfork had a long stick with a metal ring at the end of it. In the metal ring was a length of raw looking rope, probably used to hang the pitchfork in the shed with? I also saw that Ryder had that maniacal looking grin on his face again.

"Hey, that's great that you got his shorts off him," Ryder said when he was standing with us. "Okay you two tit hungry lugs, enough with those nips of his for the moment. Get those under shorts of his down. I'll give you guys' three guesses where I'm going to put this pitchfork. Alex and Ronald reluctantly peeled their lips off my nipples, giving my nubs a few final licks, sucks and kisses. They pulled my briefs down around my thighs, revealing my big, throbbing, fat manhood. My cock pointed straight up at the sunny sky, pre cum oozing out of the tip of it, and sliding down my veiny shaft.

"Man, lookit the size of that whopper," Alex said in awe, drinking in the sight of my huge cock. "His fucking schlong looks like it has a load and a half and then some stored up in it...bet it would take a while to milk this fucker dry...and then some..."

For a split second I thought of Gabriel and Howard and how they had had such a grand old time doing just that, namely milking me dry...how funny they would have no doubt found all this.

"Got a lot of spunk stored up in these testicles eh TJ?" Alex asked me and gave my family jewels a tug and shake, as if he were ringing church bells.

Then, Ryder stepped behind me with the pitchfork in hand and I cringed as he squatted down back there. I thought for sure he was going to stick me with the pitchfork and leave me out here for the vultures to feed on.

"Okay scumbag, spread those sexy legs apart and show me those family jewels…" Ryder said sternly, giving my ass cheeks a few hard slaps.

Shaking in total fear I did as I was told, exposing my big dangling balls between my thighs for him. Ryder grabbed my nut sac, hooked the length of rope at the end of the pitchfork around them, pulled the rope tight, and let go of the pitchfork. The pitchfork then lay in a diagonal position from my poor balls to the ground.

"There, now you can plow the ground as you walk, or crawl," Ryder said, giving the pitchfork a tug, getting a loud yelp of pain out of me. My balls were pulled agonizingly under my ass crack and the raw rope on the pitchfork irritated them miserably.

"Damn man Ryder, that's a real, fucked up thing to do to a guy's balls," Alex said, giving one of my nipples a hard squeeze.

"And this is just the beginning…" Ryder said and for a moment slammed his face against my ass and sniffed my hole real heartily.

I involuntarily lifted myself to my tiptoes for a second as the ruggedly handsome cop sniffed my shit chute…

"Come on, let me show you guy's around…" Ryder said and with that he took the handcuffs off my wrists.

"Okay asshole, you're about to find out why I just freed

your hands…"Ryder said, hooking the handcuffs back onto his belt. "Try anything stupid, and I mean *anything,* and you will be sorrier than you already are…"

Ryder gave me a hard swift kick behind my knees, sending me to my knees, falling with my hands reflexively out in front of me.

"OOOOOFFF…" I gasped as I hit the ground hard.

"Okay asshole, let's move it…" Ryder said, stepping in front of me, prepared to lead the way. "You two, help him along… and you know what the fuck I mean…"

Alex and Ronald found some long pieces of fallen tree branches as Ryder started walking toward the farmhouse with me crawling behind him. That pitchfork tied to my poor balls dragging behind me only slowed me down…until Alex and Ronald started whipping the fuck out of my butt with the long pieces of tree branch that is. I yelped miserably each time they rapped my butt good and hard with the branches. That sure got me moving let me tell you. A few times they meanly and mockingly poked at my ass crack with the branches, really getting some wails of pain out of me. As I crawled along behind Ryder my hands were getting all muddy and filthy, my knees were becoming more scraped up, and my balls, god, my balls were feeling worse and worse with each passing second.

"Move along there Doggy!!" Alex yelled gleefully and gave my ass a hard whack with his piece of tree branch.

I cried out in pain and Ronald gave me another hard whack, followed by two more from Alex. I was starting to sweat already.

"Plow that ground for me asshole…"Ryder said cheerfully

as I pulled that pitchfork along with my balls.

Finally, after what seemed like forever and after endless whacks to my butt cheeks we were in front of the rundown looking farmhouse. Ryder stepped in front of me, his shiny boots mere inches from my trembling lips.

"On your feet asshole…"Ryder said sternly.

Before standing up I slowly moved my face toward one of Ryder's boots. When he didn't do anything to stop me I leaned down and pressed my lips against one of his boots and gave it a hard syrupy kiss.

"Damn Ryder, despite it all I think this slob is in love with you…" Alex said and whacked my ass hard with his piece of tree branch.

"OWWWWRRR!!!" I roared in pain.

"YEAH?" Ryder asked. "Well, he won't love me so much when he sees the chore he's about to undertake."

I slowly got to my feet and stood there sweating, panting, and just looking totally miserable and afraid as the three cops looked me over mockingly, showing no compassion. When I felt the strange sensation on my cock I looked down and saw that there was a big old horse fly on the tip of it.

"YAHHHH!!!" I screeched and shooed the fly off my cock.

It flew off and the three cops stood there laughing at the sight of me standing there with my briefs curled stupidly around my thighs and the pitchfork dangling off my poor balls.

"Just a fly asshole…"Ryder said, giving the tip of my cock

a pinch. "Believe me; it's going to get a lot worse before this day is out...the way I'm going to have you sweating the fucking mosquitoes and other insects will be feasting on you and eating you alive..."

I looked at him in anguish...

"Now, you see all those big pieces of wood piled up next to the house Mr. John?" Ryder asked me, pointing in the direction he wanted me to look.

I saw what he was pointing at...stacks and stacks of old splintery looking two by fours all piled up against the side of the farmhouse. I looked at Ryder and nodded, not saying a word.

"What I want you to do is take all those pieces of wood, a few at a time, over your big strong shoulders, and carry them into the barn," Ryder said to me, sneering scornfully. "In the barn I want them piled up against the side wall..." "Damn Ryder, by the time he's done those shoulders of his are going to be all scraped and sore..." Alex said giving one of my wounded ass cheeks a squeeze.

"So they will be..." Ryder mused. "So they will be... Come on guys; let's stack some two by fours across Mr. John's broad shoulders."

Ryder took me by the arm and we all walked over to the stacks and stacks of wood.

"You ready for some real hard work scumbag?" Ryder asked me, squeezing my arm hard. "You ready to fucking sweat like a pig?"

I simply nodded.

"Because this is only the beginning you asshole..." Ryder said threateningly. "This is only the warm-up to the big stuff..."

A few moments later I was standing there with three long pieces of wood slung across my shoulders, courtesy of the three cops.

"Okay asshole; get those pieces of wood into the barn... fast!!" Ryder barked at me. "Then get back here on the double... there'll be plenty more waiting for you..."

The cops all gave my nipples a hard squeeze each, sending chills through me and then I was walking slowly toward the barn with the wood slung across my shoulders...dragging that pitchfork behind me with my aching balls.

"Move it you asshole!!" Alex yelled, came running up behind me, and gave my ass a hard whack with his piece of tree branch.

"OWWWRRRR!!!" I roared in pain, anger and helplessness.

I made it to the barn with the wood, walked inside, and laid the three pieces of wood against the wall, just as Officer Ryder had instructed me to do. I walked out of the barn, the rope around my balls aggravating me with each step I took.

"Damn, he looks miserable with that pitchfork dragging behind his ass Ryder..." Ronald said.

"And he's going to look even more miserable before this long day is over..." Ryder said. "Come on Mr. John, get a move on!! Lots of wood waiting to be carried into the barn."

When I got back to where the three cops were standing

they quickly loaded another four heavy slabs of wood across my shoulders.

"There you go asshole..." Ryder said, giving my ass a hard slap. "Get them into the barn with the other ones, and then hurry up back here."

As I walked slowly toward the barn a second time with the wood slung across my shoulders I was sweating like a stuck pig. I felt a tingling on my chest, looked down, and saw that a few big flies were making their way across it. One of the flies landed on one of my nipples, sending chills through me. Obviously the fly on my nipple had been lured by the sweet scent of saliva there. I grimaced when I felt insects crawling up and over my ass cheeks as well. I quickly squeezed my ass cheeks together for fear that the insects would somehow crawl up inside me...

I made it to the barn a second time, squatted down, and put the wood with the first stack I had brought in. I stood up, shooed the insects off me, and began walking back over to the cops, sweat dripping off me everywhere. What a sight I must have been...my damned under shorts still curled around my thighs, a fucking pitchfork trussed to my balls being dragged behind me, and me all sweaty and suffering, wearing my sneakers and sweat socks... When I got back over to the cops not a word was spoken this time. They simply loaded more wood across my shoulders. I turned and began making my way toward the barn again. I placed the wood in the barn, walked back over to my captors, and had more wood slung across my shoulders. This time as I was walking toward the barn with four slabs of wood across my shoulders the heat became too much for me and I buckled...falling halfway to my knees in a squatting position.

"UHHHHNNNFFF..." I gasped, holding tightly to the wood bearing down heavily on me.

"Want me to get him moving?" Alex asked Ryder, lifting his piece of tree branch.

"No, I want to see what he does..." Ryder said. "Come on Mr. John, get moving!!"

I took a deep breath, gripped the wood tighter with my fingers, and heaved myself to my feet. I walked to the barn with the wood and set it down with the other slabs.

"Alex, go to your car and get the cooler," Ryder said as I was walking back toward them, prepared to haul more wood.

"You want the cooler with the drinks or the one with the food?" Alex asked.

"The drinks..." Ryder said, his attention focused on me as I slowly approached, sweating horribly.

Alex walked off to the cars as Ryder and Ronald piled four more slabs of wood across my now scraped up and aching shoulders.

"When you get back this time there'll be a nice cold drink waiting for you Mr. John..." Ryder said, giving my ass a hard squeeze, twisting the handful of flesh as he did so. "Now, move it..." I walked back toward the barn with the new pieces of wood across my shoulders. By now my balls were all swollen and aching like I cannot even describe from the dragging of that pitchfork along with me...

Unfortunately things were going to get worse very soon...

I put the wood down in the barn and slowly made my way back to the three men. When I reached them Alex was standing there, a big blue cooler at his feet. Ryder leaned down, opened the cooler, and took out a quart-sized bottle of mineral water.

"Okay Mr. John, time to cool down a bit..." Ryder said as I approached. "Don't want you dying of thirst on us...still too much work to be done around here..."

All thee men laughed at Ryder's bad joke. I got to where they were standing and stood facing Ryder, waiting for him to hand me the bottle of cool water...my lips was trembling just at the thought of the cool delicious liquid.

"Thirsty Mr. John?" Ryder asked me.

I nodded and Ryder smiled.

"Get on your knees and ask me properly for a drink..." Ryder said sternly.

I slowly slid to my knees in front of Ryder, the pitchfork tugging mercilessly on my poor balls. My head hanging down I leaned forward and kissed the tips of each of his boots before looking up at him...

"P-please Officer Ryder, Sir," I said softly. "I-I'm so thirsty Sir...may I please have a drink...Sir?"

Ryder smiled with total satisfaction and handed me the bottle of mineral water.

"Sip it asshole, don't gulp it down..." Ryder instructed me.

"Y-yes Sir..." I replied my hands shaking as I took the cap off the bottle.

I put the bottle to my lips and sipped it…delicious, to say the least.

"Cool him down a little more Ronald…" Ryder said as Ronald was also sipping a cool bottle of water.

Ronald stepped over to me and for a moment I thought he was about to pour the contents of his water bottle over my head. Instead, he yanked out his huge cock and pissed atop my head as I drank water. I didn't utter a single word of complaint…hell, I knew that if I did Ryder would make me suffer horribly for it… more-so than I was already suffering already too. I simply knelt there with my head hanging down as Ronald baptized my back now by pissing on it…

"You have to piss Alex?" Ryder asked.

"Yeah, maybe a little…" Alex said and pulled his cock out, aimed it over my wounded shoulders and let go with a small yellow stream, burning my scraped up shoulders.

"When you're done with your water I'll piss also…" Ryder said.

When my bottle was empty Ryder pulled his oversized cock from his uniform pants. I tilted my head back, dropped my mouth open, and waited, prepared to gulp down Ryder's piss.

"Damn Ryder, you got this fucking guy trained real well…" Alex said as Ryder pissed in spurts in my mouth.

"Sure as shit," Ryder said with a grin. "Sure as fucking shit…"

When Ryder was done pissing I looked longingly at his huge cock as he packed it back into his uniform pants.

"Yeah I know what you want asshole," Ryder said mockingly. "But you're going to wait for that. Now, on your stinking feet!!"

Holding my empty water bottle in hand I got myself slowly back to my feet.

"Alex, could you do something with Mr. John's empty water bottle?" Ryder asked, looking mockingly at me as he spoke.

"Sure thing man..." Alex said, taking the plastic bottle from me. "Spread those legs hot guy..."

I gulped in total fear, but did as I was told. I leaned over, spread my legs wide, and Alex began inserting the bottle slowly up my ass...the thin front end first.

"AAAARRRHHHHHH!!!" I gasped loudly, leaning over with the palms of my hands resting on my thighs. "OOOHHRRRRRRR!!!"

"Ha!! Bet that feels real good eh Mr. John, that bottle being shoved up your damned shit chute..." Ryder joked, reached down and gave my nipples a good hard squeeze each.

"AAAAYYYYYYRRRR!!!" I reeled and my head spun as the bottle was forced still further into my hole, it being rotated as it went...inch by painful inch...driving me batty...

"AAAAAAYYYRRR!!!" I screeched when the bottle was just about halfway in my hole.

I didn't think it could go any further but Alex was persistent I'll give the guy that. He rotated the bottle a bit more and then I heard a horrible popping sound as the bottle was forced just about all the way up into my innards.

"OOOOOOOOOOO…" was the sound I made as my eyes crossed in my head.

"Okay Ryder, you sadistic shit, the bottle is in his shit shaft, and going nowhere," Alex said, giving my ass a hard slap.

"Straighten up now Mr. John," Ryder said, letting go of my nipples.

I slowly stood up straight, my arms dangling at my sides, sweating and panting. The feeling of that infernal water bottle wedged up inside me was phenomenally awful, like nothing I had ever known before. My cock was (fear) hard as a rock and aching miserably between my legs.

"Looks to me like he's enjoying having that bottle crammed up in his asshole…" Ronald said, looking at my throbbing horse-meat.

"Sure does at that…" Ryder said. "Tell me Mr. John, do you like having that bottle stuck up in your stinking hole?"

"N-no Sir…Officer Ryder…I-I don't Sir…" I said through trembling lips.

"Well, that's just too fucking bad, because that's where the fuck its going to stay…till I say otherwise that is…" Ryder said to me as Alex and Ronald tweaked my nipples. "You ready to haul more wood into the barn Mr. John?"

"Y-yes Sir, if you say so Officer Ryder…" I responded breathlessly.

Ryder simply smiled and then he and his two buddies all reached for a slab of wood. In moments I had four heavy two by fours slung across my aching shoulders. Carrying the wood with that pitchfork tied around my balls and dragging behind me was bad enough...but now, with that bottle crammed up in my hole it made my situation even worse. Damn, Ryder hadn't been kidding when he had told me that he was my worst nightmare come to life... I trudged miserably toward the barn with the wood slung across my poor aching shoulders... As I slung wood back and forth from the house to the barn I thought back to how it had all finally ended up at the gym. The morning after Gabriel and Howard had left me trussed up in the locker room my two buddies Jerry and Ralph had found me...

It was now six fifteen in the morning...fifteen minutes past opening time at the gym...and I was still tied to the post in the locker room as my two buddies, Jerry and Ralph went on licking me, everywhere.

"Ohhhhhrrrr..." I moaned helplessly. "Shitheads! Shouldn't one of you clowns be up at the front desk? Gym members will be arriving soon after all..."

"Members don't start arriving till between six thirty and six forty five my delectable TJ," Jerry said as lapped my juicy balls, which were sticking out of my sweat and cum soaked briefs. "Besides, Linda will be up there in a few minutes and she has front desk duty this morning. Damn, but your balls taste real musty and sweaty TJ."

I stood there helplessly as my two so called buddies sucked my sore nipples, licked my balls, and stole sucks on my cock. As for duty at the gym my duties had ended at ten PM the night before...and I was still trapped there and being used like a cheap whore... As a final joke Gabriel and Howard had left me tied to a damned post in the center of the locker room. They had just finished getting dressed and I was about to take a shower when Gabriel piped up about another thought he just had, looking at me fiendishly as he said it and from that look I just knew I was in for more nastiness. I wondered miserably if he was planning on forcing me through some more horrendous workouts, because if he was there was no way I would be able to see it through, not after what I had been forced through already.

"WH-what exactly do you have in mind now???" I asked him nervously.

Gabriel looked at Howard and the two men smiled evilly at each other.

"Howard, by any slight chance, do you have some rope in your gym bag?" Gabriel asked his buddy with a sly look on his face.

"Yes, by slight chance I do…"Howard responded, grinning from ear to ear.

"No, no…" I whispered as Howard fished a mound of rope out of his gym bag.

I was still thinking they were going to make me workout some more. Instead, they grabbed me quickly by my arms and stood me against a concrete post in the center of the locker room. In practically no time at all I was roped tight to that post… helpless.

"You bastards!!" I yelled at the two yuppies. "What's the point of this now???"

"The point TJ is that when whoever opens this gym in the morning is going to find one very beat to shit, one very sexy gym instructor here," Gabriel said jokingly, trailing the tip of one finger over my sweaty chest. "Come on Howard, let's get going. It is late after all. Good night TJ, it's been real…"

They each gave my nipples a departing squeeze and walked toward the stairs which led up to the exit.

"BASTARDS!! Untie me you guys!!" I roared angrily as they left the locker room. "What a fucked up way to leave me after all you did to me! GAWD!!!"

"Don't worry TJ; we'll lock up on our way out..." Gabriel called back to me.

"RRRRRRR!!!" I seethed in utter frustration.

So, for the rest of the hours of the night I remained tied to that post, totally unable to get myself loose. What with the way I had been forced to workout it was no wonder my strength was totally sapped. At six AM my two CO-workers, Jerry and Ralph found me. And so, there I was, tied to that damned post as my two so called buddies licked and sucked me like I was a human ice cream cone. When this would end was not in sight for me. I was exhausted both physically and mentally at that point, yet my cock was hard as a fucking rock as they worked on me.

"Man TJ sure looks real beat Jerry," Ralph said. "Maybe we should give him a break at this point."

"Yeah, you're right, we want to be considerate of the poor guy after all, he's been through hell and back," Jerry said, grinning. "I know; let's stash him in the steam room while we finish our morning opening chores. Then we'll come back down here and work on him some more..."

"No, no, *no...*" I whispered breathlessly as they slowly untied me from the post. "I need to get home and get some sleep...I-I've been up all fucking night..."

"You sure have been..." Ralph said, giving my hard cock

a grab and a twirl. "You're really up down here TJ."

When I was untied from the post they held me tightly by my arms and walked me quickly to the steam room.

"Guys please," I whimpered, trying desperately to pull out of their strong grasps.

But alas, it was no fucking use. I was too tired and too spent to do anything to defend myself. I was going into the steam room whether I wanted to or not... In the steam room they stretched me out on the long table on my back and turned the steam up full blast. I lay there half asleep and half awake as my two buddies went to do their work. The steam caressed my tired, sore, and aching body and my muscles felt relaxed after a few minutes. It turned out that a good steaming was what I really needed at that moment. However, I was still trapped because the heat kept me practically paralyzed atop that table. A short while later the steam went off and Ralph and Jerry returned. Upon entering the steam room they immediately and anxiously went back to work on me. They sucked my cock till it was sore and squeezed a good load of jazz out of me, making me sing a moaning symphony in the bowels of the steam room. That done they sucked my toes, my nipples and lapped hungrily at my balls...hard. I grunted and groaned in a mixture of a real guy's pain and utter ecstasy, begging them to stop, yet at the same time not wanting them to stop as I lay there gripping the sides of the table. What a combination of feelings eh? Finally, oh God, finally, they stopped, they stopped and helped me to the shower room. I pulled my sweaty and stinking briefs off and stepped into a shower stall. I stayed in there for about fifteen minutes or so, really letting the warm water cascade over my aching body. I don't think I was ever so tired as I was at that moment. When I was done in the shower I walked slowly back to the locker room. A few members were there, getting changed for their morning workouts. Good God almighty, just the thought of working out right then made me edgy. I had visions of some of the early morning yuppies who were now there jumping me and forcing me through another hard and treacherous workout. I opened my locker, got dressed, (minus my socks of course) and exited the gym…not even saying good-bye to Ralph and Jerry. At home I fell into bed with my clothes still on and slept almost thirteen hours…

While I was still working at the New York gym as an instructor/personal trainer I saw Gabriel and Howard one more time. It was an evening a few weeks ago. They did not get the drop on me again, but I could tell from the way that they looked at me that night that they definitely wanted to work me over again. I was not ready to be worked over that way again any time soon… Ralph and Jerry never mentioned what they had done to me the morning they had found me tied up in the locker room, but, like Gabriel and Howard I could tell that they were ready for another good go at me.

It was an hour and a half, to two hours later when I was finally done hauling the wood into Officer Ryder's barn. Tired, aching, and sweating I knelt before the three men, sipping another bottle of mineral water.

"Hope one of you guys thought to bring some food…" Ryder said.

"I have a cooler with sandwiches and stuff in the back seat of the car…" Ronald responded. "Just like an old fashioned picnic, har, har!! You want to eat now?"

Ryder looked at his watch and said "no", adding that he had a job he wanted done in the barn. I knew what that meant.

"Hurry up and finish drinking that water Mr. John…" Ryder said, poking my knee with the tip of his boot. "We're all going in the barn next…you have another heavy duty job waiting for you in there…" A few moments later I finished my water. Ryder had Alex take the pitchfork off my now swollen and very sore balls, and he also yanked the water bottle out of my hole. It came out with a squishy sound and my hole felt somehow lonely once it was out. Ryder slung me up over one of his big shoulders and carried me like a sack of potatoes toward the barn, his hand firmly pressed against my butt…

"What are you going to have him do in the barn Ryder?" Alex asked anxiously, sounding very much like he was starting to enjoy all this.

"I have a shit load of bales of hay strewn all over the floor in there…" Ryder replied as he carried me with seemingly utter ease. "This stack of shit is going to sling them up to the upper section of the barn and pile them up real neat and organized like…"

As he spoke Ryder slid two of his big thick fingers into my hole, prodding it at the same time, digging in there.

"OOOOOOO…" I moaned as my head hung down over his back.

"You guys ever watch another guy sling bales of hay?" Ryder asked his two buddies as we neared the barn.

"No man, we haven't…" Ronald responded.

"It really works a guy's muscles hard, hard to the point that it's awful after only slinging about five or six bales of hay…" Ryder said fiendishly as we entered the barn. "And as you guys can see there are about twenty to thirty bales of hay in here…"

At the sound of that I moaned in sheer anguish…

As Ryder's two buddies snickered meanly Ryder slid his fingers out of my hole, let loose his grip on me, and I slid to the floor hands first. When I hit the floor of the barn I instantly pulled myself to my knees in front of the muscle bound ruggedly handsome cop. Despite my situation it felt natural somehow to be on my knees in front of this big cop.

"Okay Mr. John, you ready to start slinging hay?" Ryder asked me as I knelt before him, looking up at him in agony.

Very slowly I nodded "Yes" and he slid his fingers that had been in my asshole into my mouth. I quickly lapped saliva on them and cleaned them off for him.

"Then get started..." he said with a sneer.

I leaned forward, leaned down, and kissed the tip of each of Ryder's boots real hard.

"Yep, despite it all the fucking guy is falling for you Ryder..." Alex said, clapping Ryder on the back. "He's falling real hard for you!" Ryder didn't say a word as I pulled myself to my feet, leaving my under shorts all tangled and comical looking around my thighs...

There was a rope connected to a pulley in the middle of the barn with a long metal hook on the end of the rope. Thankfully the bales of hay were all tied securely with mounds of rope so all I would have to do is put the bales of hay onto the hook and sling them up to the upper section of the barn...and then run up there and stack them neatly...about thirty fucking times...no big deal buds! I wiped my sweaty hands on my under shorts and lifted the first bale of hay, carrying it over to the hook on the rope. My cock was still hard, pointing straight up at the ceiling, and oozing a mess of pre cum as I worked...

"Jeez Ryder, he has one hell of a pumped up muscular body," Alex said as the three men leaned against a wall, watching me intently as I began hoisting the first bale of hay upwards. "Great looking too… almost as handsome as a movie actor…you really found yourself one hell of a guy…"

Ryder looked at Alex with a blank expression on his face. Alex simply smiled and tugged Ryder's tie. I worked hand over hand, hoisting the first bale of hay to the upper section of the barn, grunting loudly as I worked. When the bale of hay was dangling at the edge of the upper section I pulled forward on the rope, getting it onto the upper floor. I quickly let go of the rope, trotted up the steps to the upper section of the barn, took the hay off the hook, and placed the bale of hay against the barn wall. I threw the hook down and stood at the edge of the upper section of the barn, looking down at my three captors. I could see that Alex's breath caught in his throat as I stood there looking down at them…practically naked with a big stalk of a hard-on between my iron-like legs. Ronald gave the bulge in his pants a squeeze as he also stood there looking up at me…

"Good work Mr. John…" Ryder called up to me, trying to act as if he was not impressed with my naked stance. "But no dawdling or showing off…get the fuck down here and get busy with the next bale of hay…"

The three men laughed as I quickly trotted down the steps… I dashed past them and over to the next bale of hay. I quickly secured it onto the hook and began hoisting it upwards to the barn's upper section.

"Think we should give him a pair of work gloves?" Alex asked Officer Ryder. "His hands will be scraped and cut raw in no time lifting and hoisting those bales… We don't want to have to take him to a hospital to get him stitched up after all. I mean, how the fuck would we explain that?"

"Sure, I think there's a pair out in the tool shed…" Ryder replied, watching intently as I hoisted the second bale of hay. "You want to go and get them?"

"On my way…" Alex replied.

"Bring a few bottles of mineral water too…" Ryder suggested. "Our boy is going to be sweating and very thirsty very fucking soon…"

"Sure thing…" Alex said.

As Alex walked toward the door of the barn he gave me a hard, open handed slap on the ass.

"OWWWRRRR!!!" I roared angrily.

"Be right back…" Alex chortled and left the barn.

I got the second bale of hay up to the upper section of the barn, pulled forward on the rope, and got it onto the upper floor. Once again I let go of the rope and went trotting up the steps.

"How many bales of hay do you think before he's really hurting?" Ronald asked Ryder.

"He's a strong fucking guy so I would venture to guess that after the seventh or eighth one he'll be pretty much in agony…" Ryder said.

"Damn…" Ronald said, hooking his fingers around Ryder's tie and nodding his head from side to side as I came back down the steps. "I wouldn't want to be him that is for fucking sure…"

As the two men talked I saw Ronald toying with Ryder's tie, tugging on it seductively. A wave of what felt like jealousy washed over me as I hooked the third bale of hay up.

"What's up with you Ronald my man?" Ryder asked Ronald breathlessly as he pulled on his tie in a very foreplay type of fashion, looking hungrily at the big cop's bulge in his uniform pants.

"Watching you put this guy through hell is really doing a number on me Ryder..." Ronald exclaimed, also breathless. "Got my nuts churning like you would not fucking believe..."

As I began hoisting the third bale of hay Ronald leaned forward and began tonguing Ryder's already shiny badge.

"That's it..." Ryder said, squeezing the back of Ronald's neck and keeping an eye on me at the same time. "Lick my badge man...this stack of New York shit got it all shined up for me earlier back at the rest stop..."

A look of anger spread over my face as I hoisted the third bale of hay up to the upper section of the barn. Ryder sneered at me as Ronald really licked the hell out of his gold shiny badge. As I got the hay onto the upper section Alex came back in with a pair of mangy looking old work gloves and a few bottles of mineral water.

"Well, well, what's going on here?" Alex asked snidely, looking at Ronald tonguing Ryder's badge.

"Give that scumbag the gloves and get your ass over here too man..." Ryder barked, holding the back of Ronald's neck in a firm grip.

Alex tossed me the gloves as I was walking up the steps and put the bottles of mineral water on the floor of the barn. I watched as Alex knelt before Ryder, kissed the bulge in his uniform pants, and began tonguing his shiny belt buckle.

"Damn..." I whispered angrily as I climbed the steps, pulling the gloves over my hands.

"Yeah, that's it you two...lick my badge...lick my belt buckle...a mean ornery cop like me likes his badge and belt buckle real nice and shiny..." Ryder panted.

I watched out of the corner of my eye as Alex and Ronald serviced the psycho cop's badge and belt buckle, my hard cock dribbling pre cum like crazy. I put the third bale of hay with the first two and descended the steps. Ryder watched me with a look of utter satisfaction on his face.

"Move faster asshole!!" Ryder called out to me as Ronald ran his hands over his uniform shirt. "There's a shit load more work around here still to be done... Then we're taking you for a nice long walk in the woods..."

All three of the cops laughed mockingly as I hooked up the fourth bale of hay...

Ryder had been incorrect when he had said that I would be in agony when I got to the seventh or eighth bale of hay. I made it past the seventh and even the eighth and ninth bales without much difficulty...but as I was hoisting the tenth bale the pain in my arms and shoulders began to become intense. I was by then sweating pretty profusely and grunting for breath, as I had not stopped once since the first bale of hay. I was thankful though for the gloves that Alex had brought me. The three cops were all leaning against the wall of the barn...watching me... Ryder had that blank expression on his face...and that ever-present bulge in his uniform pants...the bulge that I wanted so badly to feast on. Alex looked like he was a tad concerned for me, probably thinking that I looked like I might collapse at any moment. Ronald was looking at me with eyes filled with lust and hunger… As the muscles in my arms bulged with each hoist Ronald looked more and more hungry for me it seemed.

Just great I thought… I'm being worked to death and this fucking guy wants to eat me alive. Ronald's eyes stayed riveted to my cock, my cock that didn't seem to want to go down, despite the horrible situation I was in at the moment.

"Damn Ryder, he's not looking so terrific…" Alex said. "You sure he can handle this?"

"He'll handle it…he's a goddamned gym instructor after all…" Ryder said blandly. "And besides, I'm sure you two can help him along…if you get my drift…"

Alex and Ronald snickered fiendishly as I got the tenth bale of hay onto the upper section of the barn. Being the smart and careful gym instructor that I am I stretched my poor aching arms and shoulders as I trotted up the steps to the upper section of the barn. It helped to ease the pain and tension that I was feeling, but not by all that much. A few moments later I was slowly hoisting the eleventh bale of hay, grunting and panting awfully. Alex and Ronald were holding those blasted tree branches in their hands. Now I knew what Ryder had meant when he had told them they could help me along… I was in for more whipping with those horrid branches. When the eleventh bale of hay was halfway up I faltered horribly, stopped hoisting it, and just stood there holding the bale halfway up. I looked beseechingly over at Ryder.

"Move it Mr. John!!" Ryder shouted at me. "Unless you want Alex and Ronald here to get you moving that is!!"

I took a deep painful sounding breath, flexed my muscles, and managed to get the bale of hay up to the upper section. I quickly climbed the steps. I cannot describe for you how badly I was aching at that point...

The whipping began when I was up to the seventeenth bale of hay...

With my hands now trembling, my arms and shoulders hurting like never before and sweat pouring off me in rivers I got the seventeenth bale of hay hooked up. As I began hoisting it horrible pain shot through my arms and shoulders at what seemed like one hundred miles an hour. I clenched my teeth, stopped hoisting the bale, and with my hands wrapped tightly around the rope I squeaked out the words *"My God..."* Alex and Ronald looked at each other, nodded their heads from side to side and slowly made their way over to me. I looked at Ryder through the tears, which had welled up in my eyes.

"Okay Sport, lets get that bale of hay up there!!" Alex said and whacked me hard across my ass with his tree branch.

"OWWWWWRRRR!!!" I roared in pain as Alex whacked me two more times.

I began slowly hoisting the bale of hay. To get me moving faster Ronald brought his tree branch down hard across my poor shoulders.

"OHHHRRRRR..." I grunted.

With the two men whacking my ass and shoulders with the tree branches I managed to get the seventeenth bale of hay up to the upper section of the barn.

"Move it, move it!!" Alex taunted me, chasing me and whacking me across the butt with his tree branch as I trotted over to the steps.

"Good work guys," Ryder said with a smile etched on his handsome face.

I placed the bale of hay with the others and walked down the steps.

"Think you still need Alex and Ronald to help you with the next bale Mr. John?" Ryder asked me.

I simply nodded my head "no."

"Then get moving!!" Ryder seethed through clenched teeth.

It amazed me how he could go from looking so regal and handsome to looking like a complete psychotic in almost the blink of an eye. I stretched my arms and walked past Alex and Ronald. I angrily hooked the eighteenth bale of hay onto the rope...

During all the hoisting, lifting and carting of the bales of hay I faltered again twice more. Alex and Ronald gleefully beat my shoulders and ass cheeks hard with their tree branches to again get me moving and working faster. When I faltered the second time Ryder held my arms tightly behind me as Alex and Ronald beat my nipples and cock and balls with just the tips of their tree branches. I hopped around and screamed bloody murder as I was tortured beyond reason. Those tree branches hitting my nipples and cock and balls were enough to practically drive me insane... When they were done beating me Ryder ordered me to hoist the final three bales of hay to the upper section of the barn. I was given a generous drink of cold water, a slap on the ass from Alex, and went to work on the twenty seventh bale of hay...

When I was (finally) done with the thirtieth bale of hay I made my way slowly down the steps from the upper section of the barn, walked to the center of the barn, and collapsed onto my knees, my head hanging down. Sweat dripped off me everywhere as I panted for breath, my poor body aching miserably.

"Damn Ryder, he looks awful..." Alex commented. "You're really putting the guy through a living hell."

"Not as bad as he's going to look..." Ryder replied, grabbing a handful of my sweat soaked hair and meanly yanking my head back.

"AAACCHHHH!!!" I bellowed.

"But, no reason why the three of us can't have some fun with him before he gets to the next chore I have in mind for him..." Ryder said, pulling my hair hard and twisting it in his fingers.

"AAAYYYRRR!!!" I screamed.

A few moments later I was hanging by my wrists from the hook that I had used to hoist the thirty bales of hay. My feet were a few inches off the floor and my head was hanging back between my stretched arms. A blindfold had been tied over my eyes and I felt three mouths working on me...driving me batty. Two of the cops were eating my tits like crazy, really slurp, slurp, slurping on them, chomping on them meanly with their front teeth, while a third mouth was eating my asshole. I didn't know who was doing what to me but I wondered like crazy which mouth was Ryder's.

"OHHHHHRRRR..." I moaned, as my aching and hard cock pounded like crazy between my legs, begging to shoot the pent-up load stored in my balls.

Unfortunately for my cock none of the men touched it. They made me hang there like that for a good twenty minutes or so as they feasted heartily on me. I moaned and groaned in mixtures of passion, pain and frustration. At that moment I did not know what was worse, being milked to the point of insanity the way Gabriel and Howard had done to me, or not being allowed to cum while being used as a sex toy. When the three cops stopped feasting upon me they cut me down from the hook, took the blindfold off me, and at Ryder's orders walked me out of the barn. Back out in the hot sun I stood with my hands behind me as Ryder looked around the farm grounds. He seemed to be lost in deep thought.

"What's up Ryder?" Alex asked him. "You about ready to have some lunch and then take this stack of shit out to the woods?"

"No, not just yet," Ryder replied with a fiendish grin. "I was just noticing how fucking high the weeds around this place have grown."

Ryder stood before me with a mean expression etched on his handsome rugged face.

"Tell me Mr. John, did you ever pull weeds before?" he asked me.

I nodded "no", that I had not.

"It sure as shit looks easy, but trust me on this one, it can become maddening after a while," Ryder said to me and looked at his two cronies. "Get those gloves off his hands. I want this New York stack of shit to pull weeds barehanded. After a while you're going to be so itchy that it will make you crazy Mr. John."

Alex and Ronald grabbed my wrists and pulled the sweat soaked ratty gloves off me. I stood there looking at Ryder miserably. Then, he grabbed my twisted up under shorts and tore them off my thighs. Then, holding my arms tightly stretched out at my sides Alex and Ronald laughed as Ryder crammed my stinking torn under shorts into my mouth, gagging me. He used the tip of his baton to really push the foul smelling garment deep into my craw.

"RRRRMMMFFFF!!!" I sputtered angrily.

"Okay Mr. John, go on into the tool shed, find yourself a big yard bag or two and get busy pulling weeds," Ryder said to me as I stood there looking totally stupid with my rancid under shorts in my mouth, my cheeks bulging so it looked like I a severe case of the mumps.

I turned and walked to the tool shed as the three cops laughed maniacally behind me.

"Man oh man Ryder, that was awful, cramming the poor guy's under shorts in his mouth," Alex exclaimed and all three of the cops laughed harder and harder.

I found a box of heavy-duty plastic yard bags, took two of them, and walked out of the tool shed. The rancid taste of my under shorts filled my mouth and slid down my throat.

"Begin at the side of the house and work your way around," Ryder said to me as I came back over to them.

I nodded and walked over to the weeded ground around the house. At the side of the house I dropped to my knees and began yanking out the weeds and depositing them in one of the open yard-bags. As I worked Ryder stepped behind me and nudged one of the tips of his boots against my bare ass. I looked up at him, wondering what was coming next.

"You have to pull them out by the root you asshole," Ryder said to me and poked the crack of my ass with his boot tip. "Get those fingers of yours deep in the dirt and yank the weeds by the roots."

I nodded my head up and down and did as Ryder said. Small insects that I did not recognize crawled up from under the dirt and over my hands as I worked. I shooed them away but there were always more to take their place. Ants crawled over my legs, my ass cheeks, and arms. I brushed them off, but before long there were more of them on me. Ryder had been right again, after a while of pulling weeds my hands started to itch like the devil. When I looked at all the weeds I still had to pull a feeling of utter dismay engulfed me. I worked with my head hanging down, sweat pouring off me everywhere, and stinking like never before in my life.

"Say Ryder, there's no poison ivy in those weeds right?" Alex asked.

"Don't know," Ryder replied. "And if there is, that's his problem huh?"

Again all three of the cops laughed at me. When I wasn't even halfway done pulling the weeds the first yard-bag was halfway full. The side of the house was looking better already though, what with the weeds slowly disappearing. As I moved along on my hands and knees the weeds seemed to get thicker and higher in spots. They rubbed against my exposed calves, my arms and my naked ass. It drove me crazy and I was itching in more spots than just my hands by that time. I grunted miserably behind the under shorts crammed in my mouth, moaning and groaning in tortured itchy agony. Ryder had been correct when he had said that the itching could become maddening. When I stopped pulling weeds to scratch myself Ronald came bounding over to me and whacked me a good hard one across the ass with his piece of tree branch.

"RRRRMMMFFFFF!!!" I gasped and fell to the ground, looking up at him uncomprehendingly.

"I do not recall Officer Ryder giving you permission to scratch you ass Mr. John!" Ronald shouted down at me. "Do you recall that?" I glanced over at Ryder who was standing there with his arms folded in front of him and I nodded "no", that he had not given me permission. My eyes filled with tears as I shook and trembled there on the ground.

"Back to work asshole!" Ronald ordered. "And maybe if you're lucky Officer Ryder will let you scratch your itchy ass!"

When Ronald stepped back over to Ryder and Alex Ryder shook his hand. I got back up on my knees and resumed pulling weeds. A few minutes passed and then I felt a small pebble strike one of my ass cheeks.

"MMMFFFFF!!!" I said and looked behind me.

"Bull's eye!!" Alex exclaimed merrily and picked up another pebble. "Okay guys, this time I'll go for his other ass cheek! Don't move guy! Just keep pulling those weeds!"

Alex flung the pebble with brute force and sure enough, it struck me hard on the other ass cheek.

"RRRMMMFFFF..." I sputtered.

"Okay Alex, my turn," Ronald said and picked up a pebble. "Right ass cheek..."

Ronald threw his pebble and it struck me just below my right ass cheek.

"MMMMFFFF!!!" I rattled angrily and yanked a handful of

weeds out of the ground.

"Oh shit, you missed Ronald; looks like you'll have to try again." Alex chortled.

Within moments the two men were taking turns flinging pebbles at my naked ass. What a fucked up thing huh? Those pebbles might have been small, but when thrown with the force that those two psychos were using it was absolutely painful and awfully stinging when they connected with my bare skin. Each time they struck me it stung like searing hell. Ryder didn't seem to mind that the two men were having their sadistic fun, just as long as I continued pulling the weeds. As I said they took turns, then they made bets on which of my ass cheeks they would hit next and the fuckers even aimed for my ass crack, using that as a bull's eye. I never felt so awful and mortified in my life buds. About forty-five weed pulling minutes later Ryder shouted for me to stop pulling the weeds and to sit up on my knees. Alex and Ronald stopped throwing pebbles. I did as Ryder had instructed. My ass cheeks were a mess of red marks and small bruises from all the pebbles they had thrown at it.

"One of you give him some water," Ryder said commandingly.

Alex got a bottle of water and trotted over to me with it. I knelt there as he slowly pulled the under shorts out of my mouth. Then, without a word or sound I sipped down the cool mineral water. My hand was trembling and filthy as I held the water bottle to my lips.

"Easy guy, you're going to make it through this," Alex whispered to me, smiling wickedly.

I didn't even nod. I simply took a few last sips of water and handed him back the bottle. Alex tucked the half-empty bottle under his arm, stuffed my damned smelly under shorts back into my mouth, and trotted back over to Ryder and Ronald.

"Okay Mr. John, resume your chores!" Ryder shouted over to me.

I turned my head and resumed pulling weeds and depositing them in the big yard bag. Alex and Ronald resumed throwing pebbles at my ass cheeks. Mosquitoes and flies feasted on me more and more and what I would not have given for some insect repellent spray at that that moment. When they landed on me I didn't even shoo them away at that point. When unidentified insects crawled up out of the ground and crawled over my hands and fingers I didn't shake them off. I seemed to have resigned myself to this awful twisted turn of events. I had thought at the time that what Gabriel and Howard had put me through at the gym could not be topped. Boy howdy was I wrong huh? I screeched loudly behind my under shorts gag when a large pebble hit me hard on my right ass cheek.

A while later the first yard bag was filled to the top. I climbed to my feet, tied the ends of the top of the bag together and leaned it against the house. I stood there admiring my work. The side of the house was now weeds free.

"Very good Mr. John," Officer Ryder said, stepping behind me and placing a hand on my shoulder. "Now get going on the rest."

He pointed to the front of the house and I looked at him blankly.

"Oh, and you have my permission to scratch those itchy areas on your body," he chortled, squeezed my shoulder hard and slapped my ass.

In moments I was busy yanking weeds and filling the second yard bag with them.

It was another hour and ten minutes or so in the grueling hot sun before I was done pulling weeds. By then I was stinking like never before in my whole sorry life. Shit, all I wanted was to be an actor. Funny how those dreams had led me to this mess. I thought how if I ever did make it real big and at some point I was asked to write my life story this incident sure as hell would stand out.

"Okay Mr. John, you did well, if I do say so myself," Ryder said. "You're the best farmhand anyone could ask for. Now, let's have some lunch, we'll have a friendly game of darts to relax us, and then we'll all head off into the woods for a nice nature walk.

The way the three cops were snickering I knew that there had to be more nastiness in store for me…

Lunch was served in the back of the house. Actually, I was fed my lunch of cold cut sandwiches and mineral water due to the fact that I was seated on my haunches on the ground with my hands cuffed behind me and a pole that was half in the ground was wedged up in my asshole. I sat, literally mounted on that damned pole as Ronald fed me my lunch and Alex lay before me sucking my big cock, his dessert it seemed after having eaten. It seemed that I had become their property, that these three psycho cops could do whatever they wanted with me. Ryder was sitting at a wooden table close to the house, eating his lunch and watching the spectacle before him. My torn up under shorts were on the table in front of him. A few times I saw him stealing sniffs of them in between eating his lunch.

"AAAHHHHRRRRRR!!!" I moaned as my cock was sucked and the pole in the ground fucked me.

Alex held me by my hips and rocked me up and down on that pole, really making it fuck me hard.

"RRRRRRR…" I roared mightily.

I craned my head back and looked up at the sky miserably, signaling Ronald that I didn't want anymore to eat. He said it was okay, forced the last bight of the sandwich into my mouth, and slurped one of my nipples into his mouth.

"RRRRRMMMMFFFF," I pouted around the food in my mouth.

Alex sucked my cock as Ronald slurped and sucked at one of my nipples, nursing on it man, teasing and tweaking the other one with his thumb and fingers. The two men rocked me up and down on that damned pole, tormenting the hell out of my poor hole.

"AAAARRRGGHHHH!!!" I panted, sitting there helplessly on my haunches as I was sucked and fucked.

Then, when I was about to cum Alex felt my cock pulsing like crazy in his mouth. He spitefully stopped sucking me, took my cock out of his mouth, and I could not cum.

"AAAAAARRRHHHH, uuuhhhhhh," I grunted miserably and squirmed awfully on that pole as it fucked me and fucked me and fucked me some more.

"HA!!" Didn't let the stud shoot his load huh Alex?" Ronald asked his buddy. "Fuck man, you do that shit every time!"

The two men knelt at my sides, sucked and slurped my nipples, and rocked me up and down some more on that pole. My head was spinning and I felt my juices churning miserably in my balls as my cock pleaded for release. I wanted to swear and curse like a captured marine at the two men but I simply grunted and groaned in misery. I knew that I would regret it deeply if I spoke without Officer Ryder's permission. I looked over at him sitting at the table as he finished eating. Despite everything he was doing to me and having done to me I was in total awe of the man. He was beyond handsome and more than beautiful. God, how I longed to suck his big meat pole for him. It was a half-hour or so later when Alex and Ronald stopped sucking and slurping my nipples. My cock had gone semi flaccid and my body and my hole was aching terribly. Ryder sauntered over to us and said that we would now have a friendly and old-fashioned game of darts, holding up six sharp pointed darts that he had gotten from in the house.

"But we don't have a dartboard," Ronald said mockingly to Ryder.

"Oh yes we do," Ryder said, looking down at me. "We sure as shit do."

With that he flung one of the darts at me. It landed hard in the top of one of my thighs.

"AAAAYYYYRRRRR!!!" I screamed in pain and Ryder yanked the dart out.

"Get him off that damned pole and up on the yard table," Ryder said meanly.

As Alex and Ronald hoisted me off the pole I watched Ryder's butt sway in his tight uniform pants as he walked toward the yard table where I was to be the dartboard. I swayed and tottered on my feet so Ronald hoisted me over one of his burly shoulders and carried me over to the table. As he carried me I was reminded of Gabriel and when he had carried me down the stairs to the locker room at the gym after the brutal workout that he and Howard had put me through. Ronald, like Ryder had done, slid two fingers into my hole as we neared the table...

A few minutes later I was atop the table with my knees tucked under my stomach area. My hands were still cuffed behind me and I was again gagged with my smelly under shorts crammed in my mouth. My sneakers had been taken off my feet and my socked feet were tied tightly together. My semi hard cock and big juicy balls were sticking out from behind my thighs. My thighs were roped together as well, preventing me from pulling my cock and balls back in between them to safety. Fucking fuck, but I was tied up like a goddamned Thanksgiving turkey. I was shaking and sweating in total fear atop that damned table.

"Okay you two, here are the rules for this dart game," Ryder said, his arm hooked around my waist. "You name the target you plan on hitting with your dart. The targets are this stack of shit's thighs, his ass cheeks, the bottoms of his feet, *and his cock and balls.*"

"RRRRMMMMFFFFFF!!!" I gasped mightily at those last four words.

"You heard right asshole," Ryder said and delivered a hard open-handed slap to one of my ass cheeks. "If you hit his cock or balls you earn a free shot, which means you get to go again before the next one of us is up. Any questions?"

Alex and Ronald nodded that they had no questions. Ryder handed each of his two buddies darts and they all stepped a few feet away from the table I was atop of.

"Okay, seeing as I was the one who captured this stack of shit I think it's just fitting that I should get first crack," Ryder said with authority in his voice. "His left thigh..."

Ryder took aim, threw the dart, and it hit me dead center in the left thigh.

"RRRRRmmmmmfffff..." I gurgled as the dart stuck in my thigh.

"Okay Alex, you can be next," Ryder said.

"His right thigh, right next to you," Alex said to Ryder. Alex took aim and threw his dart. It landed in my right thigh but didn't stick there. It fell to the table.

"RRRRRmmmmffff..." I sputtered angrily.

"Shit, almost had it," Alex said dejectedly. "Your turn now Ronald..."

"Those socked feet of his sure look good enough to eat," Ronald said lustfully. "I'm going for the bottom of his right foot."

As Ronald mentioned my socked feet I thought again of Gabriel and Howard. Somewhere those two guys each had one of my sweat socks I had been wearing when they captured me in the gym locker room.

Ronald threw the dart with massive force. It landed hard in the meaty bottom of my right socked foot.

"MMMMFFFFF!!!" I murmured loudly in pain.

"YEAH!!" Ronald roared happily.

"Okay guys, his left thigh again, right under my first dart," Ryder said and threw the dart.

The dart landed directly on the side of Ryder's first one.

"GGGGRRRRRMMMMFF…" I sputtered as I lay there helplessly.

"His right ass cheek," Alex said merrily and took aim.

I shut my eyes tight and waited for the impending sting. I didn't have to wait long as Alex's dart hit me dead center in the right ass cheek.

"RRRRMMFFFF!!!" I gasped and stuck my ass higher up in the air, the dart sticking out of my cheek, a comical sight in a way, but not comical for the poor guy it was being done to.

"His left ass cheek," Ronald announced and threw his second dart.

It landed on its intended mark. I sputtered angrily in pain and humiliation. The three men sauntered over to the table and collected their darts, pulling them out of my thighs and ass cheeks. I felt tiny trickles of blood oozing from the spots where the darts had penetrated my skin.

"Okay guys, lets get this game done soon," Ryder said, placing a hand on one of my ass cheeks. "I want to take him out to the woods for a long walk and some real fucking working over."

"Done deal," Alex said and Ryder gave my ass cheek a hard slap.

When they were again ready to start throwing darts at me for the next round I shuddered when Ryder announced his intended target. "The shaft of his cock," Ryder said and took aim.

Alex and Ronald seemed to hold their breath as Ryder

lined up my cock shaft with the point of his dart. He threw it. I screamed in bloody agony behind my gag, large tears flowing from my eyes and onto the table.

"Mmmmmmmmmfffff!!!!" I cried.

"YES!!!" Ryder chortled. "Now I get a free second shot, policeman's rules! His right ass cheek!!"

Ryder threw the dart and it stuck deep and all the way into my right ass cheek.

"MMMMMFFFF…" I whimpered.

"His nuts," Alex said and took aim.

I shook uncontrollably on the table at the impending pain. However Alex missed his dart landing in my right ass cheek next to Ryder's instead. I was somewhat relieved.

"Sorry Alex, you don't get a free second throw," Ryder said.

"That's okay, I can wait till my next turn," Alex replied, looking hungrily at my huge juicy sweat soaked nut sac.

"My turn," Ronald said. "I'm going for his nuts."

I squeezed my eyes shut and the dart hit home. I felt a horrible pressure on my nuts and then the dart fell to the side of the table. I thanked God for small favors as the dart did not remain wedged in my nut sac.

"RRRRRRmmmmmfffff!!" I warbled.

"Do I still get a free throw even though it fell to the table?"

Ronald asked Ryder. "I mean, it did hit his nuts after all."

"Go for it," Ryder responded. "Policeman's rules…"

Ronald aimed his second dart at me.

"His left foot this time," Ronald said and threw the dart. "For some reason I do so love those feet of his…"

The dart landed in the heel of my left foot and stuck there.

"RRRRRRRFFFFF…" I gagged.

"Okay Alex, finish it up with your last dart," Ryder said.

"Okay, his cock shaft, right under yours," Alex said and took aim.

He threw the dart and it landed in my cock shaft, just below the crown.

"RRRRRRMMFFFFFFFF!!!" I screamed loudly and thought that I would surely pass out from the awful pain.

The three deranged cops came over to me and quickly pulled the darts out of my poor cock, my foot, and my ass cheeks. I lay there whimpering in anger, fear, and pain. Ronald leaned down and pressed his nose and mouth against the bottoms of my tied black-socked feet.

"MMMM!!!" Ronald murmured. "I just knew that his socks would smell rancid. Say Ryder, when we're all done with this guy let me have these stinking socks of his, okay?"

"Sure, I suppose that that's a reasonable enough request,"

Ryder said, stepping in front of me and pulling my under shorts out of my mouth. "After all I'm going to have him, so you can have his socks."

At the sound of Ronald's sleazy request I again thought of Gabriel and Howard. Ryder took me by a handful of my hair and lifted my head up off the table. He smiled wickedly at me from ear to ear.

"Isn't that right Mr. John?" Ryder asked me. "You're going to belong to me forever after this."

With tears in my eyes I simply looked at him blankly.

"I think it's safe to say that you've earned this," Ryder said, sliding his zipper down on his uniform pants.

Alex stood caressing my ass cheeks, Ronald licked and sniffed the bottoms of my stinking socked feet, and I opened my mouth wide to receive the joy of Ryder's giant met pole. He wagged the enormous thing in my face and then slipped it inch by inch into my eager mouth. I sucked it in with real zeal and utter gusto.

"OHHHHHHRRRR yeah, suck my big meat you fucking stack of shit," Ryder grunted and ran a hand through my hair.

As I sucked and suckled him for all I was worth Ronald licked feverishly at the bottoms of my feet and sucked my toes. Alex spanked my ass cheeks and even ran his tongue across them a few times, giving my cock a few good tugs, sending chills of ecstasy through my tortured body.

"Heh, heh, maybe I'll let you get off this time," Alex chuckled. "Suck Officer Ryder's cock."

Fuck that, I didn't need to be told twice. Ryder's cock in my mouth was awesome. It somehow made all he had put me through worth it. His cock literally filled my mouth and it seemed to swell more and more as I sucked him and sucked him. My cheeks bulged with his girth well into my craw. I poked my tongue into his large cock slit and twirled it around in there, driving the cop crazy. He bucked his muscular body forward in a sexy fashion as he forced his cock into my throat and threw his head back. It was the most vulnerable that I had seen him look since he had captured me. He choked me with his cock as Alex stroked mine behind my thighs. (That felt beyond awesome let me tell you.)

"Ohhhhhrrrr yeah, getting there now you New York stack of shit," Ryder gasped, grasping the handful of my hair even tighter. "Oh yeah, getting real close you cock sucker."

Then, Officer Ryder, hung like a horse cop, spewed forth a mess of cum the likes of which I had never known or felt before. He spewed his glorious massive mess of cop's cream into my mouth and down my throat, making sure that I didn't lose a drop of his precious liquids.

"Ohhhhhrrrr yeah, yeah, swallow my load you cock sucker," Ryder grunted as he continued fucking my mouth as he seemed to just cum and cum and cum and cum some more.

His balls just seemed to be pumping out loads upon loads of his good stuff as he fed it to me. Ropes upon ropes of his thick creamy sperm filled my mouth and I gulped and heaved it down as if I was in a chugging contest of some sort.

"Oh yeah Ryder, shoot that load man," Alex said as my cock pulsed in his hand. "Feels like this guy is getting close to popping his load as well."

Then, again, that scumbag Alex let go of my cock, preventing me from shooting my load.

"RRRRRRRR..." I grunted angrily as my harder than hard cock slapped back against my thighs.

Ryder's cock slipped from my mouth as my own juices retreated and churned around in my suffering balls.

God Alex, if that was me you did that to twice I would beat the living fucks out of you," Ronald chortled as he held onto my socked ankles.

"Yeah, poor guy is aching to shoot his load at this point," Alex chuckled meanly and squeezed my balls hard.

"AAAARHHHH..." I gasped.

"Time for a walk in the woods you two," Ryder said, packing his spent cock back into his uniform pants and zipping up. "Ronald, untie his feet and take his socks. They're yours. This guy is going to walk barefoot through nature's unforgiving wilderness.

As Ronald untied my feet and peeled my very rancid socks from them I looked up at Ryder helplessly. The sweet taste of his ball juice was still in my mouth.

"Yeah, a real nice walk in the woods with us and nature," Ryder said, cupping my chin in his hand.

Looking at me somewhat longingly he stuck the tip of his thumb in my mouth and without being told to I kissed it. Then we looked at each other intensely for a few seconds before I was taken off the table and stood on the ground on my bare feet. I was totally naked at that point.

"Okay guys, lets get ready," Ryder said.

Within moments the cops all had backpacks filled with supplies on their backs. Alex took a pair of sharp-teethed tit clamps from his pocket and clipped the mean looking things tightly onto my well-sucked and very chewed up nipples.

"AAAARRGGHHHH!!!" I gasped as the tit clamps bit awfully into the tender flesh of my poor nipples.

"Tell you guy, you'd better hope upon hope that I don't jack you off and leave those things on you after you've shot your load," Alex said to me tauntingly. "If you're like most guys your tits most likely become super sensitive after you've shot a load, especially a load as big as the one you're carrying around in those big balls of yours. The last thing you'll want is anyone touching your tits, let alone having a pair of tit clamps on them."

"Okay guys, enough talk, lets go," Ryder said, taking me by my upper arm.

With Ryder and I in the lead we all walked into the woods. The tit clamps drove me crazy with pain and helped in a way to keep my cock painfully erect and aching to shoot that load that Alex was teasing me with. Within ten minutes or so of walking my bare feet were scraped up and cut in spots as well. Ryder was merciless though, pulling me along with him as we went deeper into the woods. From behind Alex and Ronald threw pebbles at my ass cheeks, slapped me with fallen tree branches across my butt, and whacked the backs of my thighs with heavy sunflowers. When we came to a pretty large and foul smelling mud puddle I tried to walk around it, but Ryder pushed me meanly into it.

"UUUHHHFFF..." I gasped in total disgust as the mud seemed to suck me in.

"Come on you weasel, walk through that muck!!" Ryder said from beside me.

He and Alex and Ronald watched with glee as I trudged slowly through the stinking mud puddle. It seemed to take forever to get to the other side of it and then work my way out. As I then trudged toward the other side of the mud puddle a big bumblebee landed on one of my clamped nipples and decided he wanted to stay there a while.

"AAAAAYYYYY!!!" I screamed at the prospect of now being stung by a bee.

"Leave it alone and it'll fly off you sniveling stack of shit!!" Ryder yelled at me. "Come on; get out of that mud already! We have a way to go yet!"

I huffed for breath and finally made my way out of the mud puddle. As I climbed out it felt like the mud was clinging to my feet and wanting to suck me back in. My calves and feet were covered in filth and the bee was still on my nipple. I could actually feel the fucking insect licking at the very tip of my goddamned tit. Smiling, Ryder whacked the bee off me, sending a jolt of pressured and searing pain through me as the tit clamp rocked and pulled on my poor nipple.

"AAAYYYRRRR!!!" I screamed, feeling like I was just about insane at that point.

Ryder took my arm and we walked on. Alex and Ronald stole hard squeezes on my ass as we plodded along. Sweat covered me from head to toe and I could smell myself by then. I was beyond ripe and awful. After a good (bad?) forty-five minutes of walking Ryder said we would stop for a break of water and to sit down. Water for me as well, but I would not be sitting. Ryder pointed at Alex and Ronald, pointed at me, and pointed at a big tree with very strong looking branches adorning it. Without being told they knew what they were to do. Unfortunately I also knew what they were to do. It took them less than a few minutes to string me up by my wrists to a tree branch that Ryder had pointed out to them. My feet just about touched the ground as I hung there like a side of beef in a butcher's freezer. Alex fed me some cool water from his canteen as Ronald tugged on the chain hanging on the tit clamps.

"AAAARRHHHH," I grunted miserably and quickly swallowed the water.

Ronald also gave me some water from his canteen then the two men and Ryder sat down on a fallen tree that was near the one I was strung up from.

"How much further do you want to walk?" Alex asked Ryder. "It's going to be late afternoon pretty soon and then it'll be getting dark."

"Yeah, don't want to be out here when it's dark," Ryder said. "Makes it difficult to find your way back."

"What are you plannin' on doing with him when we get back to the city?" Ronald asked Ryder.

Ryder looked me over before responding.

"Fuck, I plan to hose him down," Ryder said smartly and the three men laughed hysterically at his joke.

"Are you going to let him go Ryder?" Ronald asked Ryder next.

"Have to man, can't keep him in storage after all," Ryder replied.

"What if he reports all this?" Alex asked.

"He won't," Ryder said and took a sip of his water. "Fucking stack of shit is crazy about me."

As I hung there my arms and shoulders began to feel more than numb. What with all the lifting of those bales of hay earlier I could not believe that my arms were feeling anything at that moment. What I didn't know was what I was in for on the walk back. Ryder and his two cronies relaxed for a few more minutes, sipped some more water, and then got to their feet.

"Okay Mr. John, are you ready for the trek back?" Ryder asked me, giving one of my tweaked nipples a squeeze. "You have my permission to reply."

"Y-yes Officer Ryder, I'm ready," I said softly.

"Got this guy trained real well," Ryder said with satisfaction in his voice. "Cut him the fuck down."

As Alex and Ronald cut me down from the tree branch Ryder was looking at a husky fallen tree branch that was lying on the ground.

"Hey guys don't put that rope away after you've cut him down," Ryder said with his back to the two men as they yanked my arms behind me and walked me over to where Ryder was standing. "I just came up with a really twisted and mean idea."

Ryder looked at me, squeezed one of my clamped nipples hard again, and smiled fiendishly.

"Oh Mr. John, by the time this is over you're going to be a new man," he said with that smile on his face.

A few moments later I was standing there with that husky fallen tree branch slung across my shoulders. The bark scraped and irritated my shoulders and the weight of it felt immense. Alex and Ronald had tied my wrists securely to the ends of the damned thing, tethering it atop my shoulders.

"Okay Mr. John, lets see how far you can get carrying that heavy load," Ryder said to me. "Let's go."

Ryder took the lead with Ronald and Alex following behind me, making sure that I was okay as I carried the big branch along with me. As I plodded along with the three men mosquitoes and flies were again feasting upon me. My hard cock had finally dwindled down to a shriveled up dick. I was tired, beaten, and totally out of my mind at that point. What they had done to me, what they were still doing to me was beyond torture. The clamps *still* on my nipples made my head spin. Walking behind Ryder I was transfixed watching his butt sway in his tight fitting uniform pants.

I made it halfway back with the tree branch lashed across my poor shoulders. It was at that point that I faltered and nearly fell.

"UUUHHHHHNNNFFFF," I gasped as I stood there tottering in place. *"C-can't..."*

Ryder turned, looked at me, and instantly ordered Alex and Ronald to get the tree branch off my shoulders. They quickly did as he said. My shoulders were all scraped and raw from the bark. For the rest of the walk back Ryder held me tightly by my arm. My hands were untied and the clamps were (finally) off my nipples. When we arrived back at the farmhouse it was late afternoon and I could see that the sun would be setting soon. Ryder walked me to the back of the house and per his word he did hose me down, thoroughly. I stood as still as possible as he turned the garden hose on me, washing the sweat, mud and grunge from my pain-filled body. The cold water felt good and invigorating as he hosed me down.

"Lean over and spread those ass cheeks for me Mr. John," Ryder commanded.

I did as he told me to do and he aimed the hose at my exposed bunghole giving it a good washing out.

"AAAARHHHHHH!!!" I roared as the cold water rushed and sluiced in my hole.

When Ryder turned off the hose I stood there soaking wet and trembling. The muscle bound cop put the hose down and slowly walked over to me. He stepped behind me and placed his huge hands on my aching shoulders, squeezed them gently and massaged them. My breath caught in my throat as he pressed his lips against the side of my neck.

"So, tell me Mr. John, is it true what my two buddies have been saying?" he asked me, his lips just about against my ear. "Is it true? Are you crazy about me despite all this?"

I took a deep breath as he gave my earlobe a hard suck.

"Answer me you fuck," he whispered meanly in my ear, grabbing my upper arms in a tight grip. "Because if you are you had better be able to take whatever the fuck I plan on dishing out on you."

He again pressed his lips against my neck. I hung my head down, still not having answered him.

"Mr. John, Thomas," he whispered in my ear, his tongue teasing the inside of my ear.

Goose bumps broke out all over me and my cock grew hard in front of me. He pulled my sopping wet body against his uniform and I felt his hard cock beneath his uniform pants pressing against my butt.

"Thomas," he whispered passionately in my ear. "*I was crazy for you the second I pulled you over on the road back there. From the look in your eyes I knew you wanted all that I could dish out on you...*"

I smiled from ear to ear, turned around, and kissed my cop hard on the mouth. What a great thing to hear, "my cop!" He squeezed my nipples and grabbed my hard cock. When Alex and Ronald came around came around to the back of the house to see what was taking so long they found Ryder standing behind me, reaching around me with my cock in his hand. They gave each other a high-five as my cop slowly jacked me off and I spewed a mess of cum the likes of never before in my life.

For the ride back to the city Ryder allowed me to sit up front with him in his patrol car. I was dressed in an old pair of jeans and a tee shirt that had been in the farmhouse and luckily they fit me. My sneakers were on my feet minus my sweat socks.

I've been in LA for over a month now. I still haven't landed that dream job as an actor yet, but working as an instructor/personal trainer at the LA gym pays the bills for the moment. Oh, did I mention that I live with Officer Ryder? Yeah, the guy really keeps me in tip-top shape. Once a month we take a ride down to his farmhouse. Thanks to all my hard work the place is really shaping up, but damn does my body ache when the day is done at the farmhouse.

The Brief Thief
(A Quick, Kinky and Sleazy Story)

"Fuck man, goddamn it, I do not fucking believe it!!" the big jock said angrily, standing in front of his locker wearing just his calf length navy blue nylon dress socks, OTC (over the calf style socks as so many high-power execs call them) executive socks I call them.

"What seems to be the problem bud?" I replied, being that my locker was just a few feet from where his was and we had spotted each other in some of our workouts earlier upstairs in the gym.

"You are not going to believe this man, but someone stole my damned under shorts," he exclaimed angrily, standing there all muscular, pumped up and still kind of wet from the shower he'd taken recently.

"You mean from right out of your locker?" I asked him, sounding real concerned.

We'd had reports of lockers being busted into at the gym I go to after all.

"No, no, not from out of my locker," he said to me, stepping a few inches closer to me as he spoke, his big meat stick dangling semi hard and his balls dangling all juicy looking between his long muscular legs. "After I'm done working out real hard I always leave my sneakers, my gym shorts, my tee shirt, my sweat socks *and* my under shorts outside my locker while I go to shower. I leave the sweaty gear piled up on the floor in front of my locker, like so many other dudes here do. I got my business suit in the locker and I don't want my gym gear stinking it up, understand?"

"Yeah, I think so," I said to him, loving the way he was standing there all handsome, rugged and at the same time vulnerable looking in just his pretty blue dress socks, totally pissed the fuck off at the same time.

He had any clue that his meat baton had grown semi hard due to his anger I don't think he really took note of it. It amazes me how so many guys lay a goddamned boner when they get really excitable and angry.

"So, anyway, this time when I got back from the shower I did what I always do," he went on. "I opened my locker, got my dress socks on, as you can see and then reached for my under shorts down on the floor...which are gone!"

He turned his back to me, stepped back over to his locker and angrily kicked the gym bag and his gym gear that was strewn on the floor in front of his locker.

"God damn it man, god damn it all," he seethed, his huge hands clenched into tight fists, his solid looking round butt cheeks gaping at me, the crack of his ass so hairy and sexy looking.

"Maybe they're mixed up in all your stuff bud, take another look," I suggested.

"Yeah, yeah," he mumbled and squatted down at his stuff.

My breath caught in my throat as he squatted there, his

legs parted and his ass cheeks spread, his big balls dangling erotically between his thighs. With just his dress socks on he made such a sexy sight that it was totally awesome. He rummaged through his gym bag, pushed his sneakers and thick white sweat socks aside and shook out his sweaty tee shirt.

"No man, they're not here," he said, getting to his feet and facing me again. "I got to tell you buddy, that that is a shitty and fucked up thing to do, to steal a guy's under shorts, off all things! Why the fuck would someone want my damned shorts?"

"Well, maybe someone really likes you bud," I said to him with a grin.

"Perverts, that's what we got at this gym, fucking sleazy perverts," he grunted angrily, again taking a few steps closer to me as he spoke.

I had all to do to keep myself from reaching out and giving his big pink fleshy nipples a friendly squeeze each. They were jutted up to the size of pencil erasers.

"Shit man, I have to get back to my office for a meeting *and* I'm going to have to free ball in my suit pants," he said, running the palm of one hand through his damp short cut dark hair.

"Maybe you could stop at a men's clothing store and buy a pair of underpants before you head back to your office bud," I suggested.

"That would be an easy solution," he said, glancing at the clock on the wall. "But shit, I'm really limited for time. Fuck it all man, I'm going to have to go into that meeting with no under shorts on under my suit. *Shit!!* Wait'll my girlfriend hears about this, she won't believe it! And of all things, she gave me those sexy drawers for my birthday, SHIT!!"

"Hey bud, it could have been worse," I said, trying to sound reassuring.

"I really don't see how," he said. "What do you mean?"

"Well, they could have snagged you socks too," I said, pointing at his dress socked feet.

"Yeah, good fucking thing I had them in my locker huh?" he asked me with a grin. "I would have looked really ridiculous going into my meeting in my wingtips with no socks on. Everyone would have seen that at the conference table when I sat down. What a thing to explain huh? But shit man, someone stole my damned under shorts!!"

By now his meat stick was rage hard and the temptation to reach out and stroke him was overwhelming.

"Hey man, there's a gym instructor just coming in here," he said, pointing at the entrance door to the locker room. "I'm going to report this little incident to him and give him a piece of my mind while I'm at it. I mean, they should have a security system here right?"

That said, he grabbed his shower towel and wrapped it around his mid section, his hard on tenting it in front.

"Hey, I thought you were pressed for time and had to get back to your office," I said to him.

"For this I'll make the time," he said and stomped angrily away from me, passing other guys as they entered and left the locker room, and over to the gym instructor who had just entered the locker room.

"Hey man, could I have a word with you?" he called out,

looking real hot wearing just the towel around his waist and his dress socks.

The guy had no fucking idea just how sexy he really was in his anger and vulnerability…

Smiling, I opened my gym bag and fondled his under shorts that were in there. Actually, they had been in there since he had gone to take his shower. I stepped over to his locker, scooped up his thick white sweat socks, sniffed them real fast, they were all musty and masculine smelling, and deposited them quickly into my gym bag along with his funky scented briefs. I zipped my gym bag closed, hoisted it over my shoulder and along with other guys headed toward the exit of the locker room, passing my new buddy and the gym instructor as they headed back toward the guy's locker.

"Fuck man, *now my damned sweat socks are gone!!*" I heard him yelling as I left the locker room, a big grin on my face.

Author's After-Word: *The short story you just read is true. A while back I had an internet chat with a buddy of mine whose name was Frank. More than anything else Frank loved playing mean jokes on unsuspecting ruggedly handsome guys. He said how the looks on their faces when they realized they'd been had was so macho and so befuddled at the time same time, something that never failed to get him going. He told me of how he had managed to snag that jock's under shorts in the gym locker room while the stud had gone to shower after his work-out. He told of how he had seen the guy in the gym and how he had started talking with him and how they got around to spotting each other on various exercise machines. Frank let the guy go down to the locker room to get showered and changed ahead of him when they were done working out. He said how this way he would have a good chance to play some sort of mean trick on the poor guy. When he got down to the locker room Frank saw the studly guy just trotting into the shower area, heading away from his locker with his back to Frank. Frank saw the guy's pile of gym gear outside his locker on the floor and snagging those under shorts was as easy as taking candy from a baby. Frank told me how the next time he saw the guy at the gym he was wearing the guy's under shorts under his gym shorts. "How kinky is that?" Frank asked me. "Very kinky, very sinister," I replied and a quick story was born. I just hope that I did Frank's experience justice in my writing of his experience. Frank never told me the stud's name so in my story I left him nameless as well...*

Bondage Buddies

"Royal flush!" I said, throwing down my cards, smiling from ear to ear. "I win, and you lose, again…"

"Goddamn it man, this is the third fucking time," my buddy Bill said miserably, throwing down what was left of his cards as I leaned back in my chair feeling real satisfied and fat-headed.

"It seems like the damned fates are really against me lately," Bill said, looking at me across the table, his eyes filled with mock despair.

"Either that or they're smiling down on me," I said, getting to my feet. "Come on; let's get you prepared while I get the box."

"Yeah, the box, the fucking box," Bill whispered, knowing all too well what "the box" meant.

I stood up, sauntered into the living room and came back with the box that we kept filled with rope and other bondage paraphernalia.

"Shit man, I really thought I had it in the bag this time," Bill said, stood up and began unbuttoning his fatigue style shirt, slipping it off followed by his olive colored tee shirt.

He neatly folded his shirts and placed them on the extra chair we kept for just hat purpose. With his dog tags dangling around his neck be bent down to unlace his bog clonky combat boots, shucked them off his size eleven feet and placed them under the chair. Watching him bend down to get his boots off always sent a shiver or two of ecstasy through me, seeing as Bill has one of the best proportioned and well muscled backs I had ever seen. The way his ripped muscles bulged and flexed while he bent over was pure magic to see.

"Looks like you win underpants again bud," he said, starting to unbutton his fatigue style pants, still all rolled up at the knees from having been tucked neatly into his boots.

"And seeing as you lost you really should be calling me Sir Soldier boy Billy," I said meanly, getting into my role rather well.

"Yes Sir, as you say Sir," Bill said. "But shit, it's sure going to feel strange going home later without my under shorts on again. Fuck man, how am I going to explain that to the wife a third goddamned time?"

"Ha, just tell her the truth," I laughed. "Tell her that you bet your under shorts in a card game and lost."

"Phooey man, I can't tell her that I gambled away my damned shorts," he said and we both laughed.

Bill had recently been honorably discharged from the army after four years and was a newly wed of only four months. Our card games however had been going on like this since we were teenagers... We always gambled on the most unusual and sleazy things that guys possibly could gamble on. When Bill told me how in the army he and his buddies had gambled on each others under shorts I could not believe it, but decided it would be fun to humiliate the hunky soldier boy, if I won that is... We made a deal that whenever we got together for our card games that Bill would come attired in his military fatigues. Whenever he lost the game I got to play POW.

A few moments later Bill was stripped to his white briefs and calf length, olive colored military issued cotton socks. From where I was standing I could tell that those socks were pretty moist having been in those boots of his for so many hours. Also, from where I was standing I could tell just how awesome they smelled as well. His muscle pipe was tenting his briefs as if Ringling Brothers had pitched a tent in his crotch area. He placed his hands behind him and stood rigidly at attention.

"Ready for your orders Sir," he said in a deep soldierly voice, the bulge in his BVD briefs starting to ooze droplets of pre cum.

"Hmm, I think that this time I'll keep your socks too Soldier boy," I said with a grin.

"Oh please Sir, how will I explain losin' my socks as well?" he grumbled miserably, beads of sweat appearing on his forehead, just under his very short cropped dirty blond hair.

"Just tell the wife that after losing your under shorts all you had left to gamble with were your smelly socks," I replied.

"Lousy way to refer to a guy's socks, shit man, third fucking time in a row that I lost at our damned card game," Bill complained.

His body was a work of United States army magic, totally rock hard and muscular, totally fucking hard bodied. The army had really turned my scrawny buddy into a brick wall. Being that Bill is a fair haired blond had no hair on his muscular torso to speak of, save for his blond pubic bush and somewhat bushy armpits. He told me once that while he was in the army he had not done well on his morning exercises and his drill sergeant had meanly shaved his pits for him as punishment. Bill recounted, sounding miserable, about how the drill sergeant had strung his wrists tight above him and tied them to a ceiling beam and then slowly and methodically shaved his pits raw. The hot water washcloths and steaming shaving cream, the highly sharpened razor, all of it still gave my buddy nightmares. It gave me a hard-on to hear him tell of it. His chest jutted out muscular and huge enough to eat a three course meal off of, that chest adorned by two big pink nipples that were always hard as pencil erasers.

"Sit down," I said sternly.

Doing as he was told Bill sat back in his chair, his hands and arms behind him and draped over the back of it. I got busy very quickly roping him to the chair.

"Shit, shit, like I said Sir, I really thought I had it in the bag this time," he said forlornly as I tied his wrists together behind him, looping the rope around and around his huge lower arms.

"The only thing in the bag Billy boy is you," I said, winding a good length of rope over his upper torso, under and over his huge male cleavage, pinning him securely to the chair.

We had been doing this sort of thing since we were teenagers, as I mentioned. Actually, it was Bill who had come up with the idea for the loser of our card games to be tied up and left that way till the winner said he could be released. I think Bill always enjoyed the fantasy of roping a guy up and then making his life miserable. I don't think however that Bill realized just how easily he could wind up the loser of the game as well. Although, as time went on I sort of got the feeling that Bill liked being tied up as well as tying me up. Each time we played he was always confident of winning. Ha, nine fucking times out of ten the poor fuck lost and lost miserably I might add. It was my idea to have the loser strip to his underwear and socks before being roped up. Bill was not crazy about that part of the game but if it meant him being able to tie me, his good buddy up, he was willing to go along with it.

The first time I jacked the guy off while I had him tied up he complained and ranted like crazy, saying that that was not part of the game, stating how we had not agreed on such folly. But after I got him off more than a couple of times he agreed to that as well, realizing I suppose, that being in bondage really floated his boat a lot more than he cared to admit.

When I finished tying his upper body to the chair Bill's muscles strained beautifully. I had left his nipples real visible and the rope tied real tight under and over them, making a nice showcase of them.

"Gods in the heavens, as fucking usual you roped me the fuck up real goddamned tight Sir," Bill seethed, straining to get himself untied but to no avail.

"Yeah, I really do love tying you the fuck up Soldier boy Billy," I said breathlessly and gave him a quick peck on the cheek, squeezing one of his erect and hard nipples real meanly as I did so.

"Hey man, hey there bud, don't be kissing me," Bill said. "This is all in good mean fun Sir. We ain't faggots here you know."

"Of course not," I said sarcastically and got busy roping his feet to the legs of the chair, spreading his legs good and fucking wide.

Bill decided to join the army when he was eighteen years old and fresh out of high school. His girlfriend Linda was sad to see him go as I was. He had been dating her for the past three years of high school and our card and bondage games had been going on for just as long. When he came home on leave the first time we played our usual game of poker. I lost once and Bill lost twice. Watching him strip out of his uniform nearly drove me over the edge. The army had done wonders in getting Bill into amazingly good muscular shape, as I pointed out; I really love pointing that out. Tying him up had never seemed more inviting at that point. I teased and taunted him about having a real POW in my clutches as I tied him up that time. When I started jacking him off he begged me to only do him once, explaining that Linda was waiting for him and she was as horny for him as a bitch in heat. I got him off twice that time and told me afterwards that when he fucked Linda later on his cock had never felt so sore. He always dreaded losing the card games because he knew that I liked keeping him tied up for long periods of time, knowing that any excuse he offered to shorten the length of bondage time would be totally ignored by me. Inwardly I knew that he loved our games. He had invented them after all. A few minutes later I had Bill's socked ankles tied to one of the chair legs each. The swelling in his white briefs was now enormous and oozing pearls and pearls of pre cum through the thin cotton fabric.

"Oh fuck man, I really cannot believe I lost that goddamned game," Bill said, straining and sweating against the ropes. "When we started I was doing so well too."

"Just goes to show what could happen Billy boy," I said and squatted down in front of him.

He watched helplessly as I slowly pulled the fly opening of his under shorts apart and almost ceremoniously brought out his rage hard cock and his big juicy peach fuzzed balls.

"OHHHHRRR fuck, just once man, please, *just once,*" Bill pleaded as I handled his gargantuan meat pole. "Linda is really, really in the mood today. I promised her that after my card game we would have an all day fuck marathon."

"Yeah, if she could only see her soldier boy husband now," I said mockingly and spit a few times onto his hardness as it pulsed like a thing alive in my hand.

Bill squirmed miserably and in ecstasy at the same time under the ropes as I began stroking his now slimy and hard meat stick

"Fuck man but my wife loves my big soldier-sized cock," Bill panted as I stroked and stroked him. *"And so do you buddy... so do you..."*

Bill's cock was of the soldier-sized as he had just referred to it, all thick, long, beefy and veiny. He never failed to shoot big hefty creamy loads for me, even after I'd jacked him off more than a couple of times. Bill married Linda shortly after his honorable discharge from the army. I was a little concerned that that would be the end of our card games. But Bill assured me that our card games were our secret and he could never give them up, always hoping against hope that he would win more often. Unfortunately for him he didn't.

"OHHHHHHRRR GODS, I-I'm getting there already buddy," Bill garbled. "Fuck. I had a goddamned hard-on while we were playing that damned game."

"Yeah, a hard-n because you thought you were going to win and tie me the fuck up," I said mockingly. "But look at you now..."

"Yeah, fucking look at me now..." Bill grumbled. "OOOHHHH FUCK, I-I'm cumming buddy, pl-please untie me when I'm done, OHHHHHRRRR FUCKING FUCKS!!!"

He threw his head back and writhed in ecstasy as I stroked his cock and squeezed his balls, getting every possible drop of soldier boy jazz from him.

"Okay Bill, I'll untie you on one condition," I said, still stroking him, getting still more jazz to erupt from his wide sexy slit.

"WH-what the fuck condition now bud?" he asked me, still panting and gasping after I'd let go of his meat stick. His mess of cum dripped down his roped up chest to his stomach area, settling on his under shorts.

"I've already agreed to give you my damned underpants and military socks," he seethed. "WH-what more do you want?"

"Another card game," I said.

"Fuck yeah, fucking A man, and this time I will win for sure," Bill said eagerly. "And then we'll see how you feel when I force you to cum more than a few times. Being jacked off is great bud, but squeezing three loads out of a guy can really get to him you know?"

I looked up at my bound buddy in shock. It would be the first time in all the years of our card games that he would jack me off.

"Don't be so sure of winning so quickly," I said, starting to untie him. "Just call Linda and tell her that you'll be a little later than expected."

"Sure thing bud," Bill said. "Right after I'm dressed."

"Well, if I were you I would stay just as you are," I said with a grin. "You never know what might happen."

"What's going to happen is I am going to win this time," Bill said with the utmost confidence, standing up and facing me.

"Whatever," I said and gave the elastic waistband of

his under shorts a snap. "But I still get your under shorts and socks."

"Yeah, yeah, damn but you got a fetish for my damned funky scented under shorts and socks," Bill mused and walked over to the phone on the wall.

He looked beyond sexy and vulnerable standing there talking on the phone wearing just his underpants, socks and dog tags. His cock was semi hard as it hung freely out of his underpants along with his big succulent balls. He explained to Linda that our card game had gotten really intense and that he would be home a little later than he had expected. After he hung up he didn't get dressed. Instead we played a second game of cards…

"Goddamn it all, *fuck, fuck,*" Bill ranted horribly and miserably a while later as I again tied him tightly to the chair.

This time to really grate on his nerves I had tied a blindfold over his eyes as well…

"Can't believe I lost again…" he seethed.

Like Most Days...

The day started out like most other days, wake up super early in the morning, shower, shave, brush the teeth, get dressed and *try* to get my ass to work on time. Like most days the 5:30 AM train was on time *and* like most days of very recently the very handsome, well dressed black guy was there. Like each day that I had seen him so far he was sharply dressed from head to toe, down to his socks and listening to his portable CD player. (These days those portable CD players have since been replaced with ipods.) The purple knit hat he always wore somehow added eroti-cally to his appearance and suave looks. Denzel Washington had nothing on this guy, at least in my opinion that is. Like most mornings I boarded the train at my stop, Bay Parkway, and took a deep breath at the sight of him as I sat down across from him. Like every morning that I'd seen him so far he was sitting with his eyes shut, his strong looking legs stretched out slightly in front of him, listening to whatever CD was his choice for that day. A few times during the ride to Manhattan he opened his eyes to glance around the train car. We'd made eye contact a couple of times. His eyes were the chestnut brown that I simply adore. I supposed his age to be in the middle to late twenties, although I'm not sure, seeing as I am pretty bad at guessing people's age. On this par-ticular day though things would be slightly different, because on this day I planned to *finally* speak with my handsome train friend. As I said, we'd made eye contact, but we had never spoken. On this notable day I planned to ask him a question that had been burning a hole in my mind for the last couple of days... (Actually he had spoken to me very, very quickly one morning a week or so ago. As I stood up to get off the train when it had gotten to my stop in Manhattan I accidentally on purpose banged the tip of my foot against his; he opened his eyes and looked at me dreamily. "Sorry," I said to him. "No problem," he replied, sounding very professional. Obviously the music wasn't up that loud. Obviously he wasn't too deeply asleep. Obviously I had a fetish for this handsome black guy's feet...)

The "B" train barreled into the station at 5:30 AM, right on time. Standing on the platform at the same exact spot that I stand each morning I saw him sitting there as the train came to a halt. He boards the train before me, though I don't know which stop he gets on at. The doors opened and I and the other passengers boarded. However on this day I did not sit across from him, instead I sat next to him, the middle seat in the three-seat space between us. Like the last few days I had seen him he was wearing black ribbed sheer socks. With his black highly shined square toed shoes, his navy blue dress pants, his light blue shirt and silk patterned tie those socks looked good enough to slobber over. It was those socks that I planned to talk to him about. It was those socks on his big feet that had driven me crazy the last few days. I imagined various pairs of them in his sock drawer, what an intimate thought... Like most days he was sitting there with his eyes shut, his headphones in his ears, listening to whatever music he had chosen for that day. With my heart pounding I glanced over at him as the train left the Bay Parkway station. His thick beautiful lips were slightly parted as he sat there either sleeping or just totally lost in the music he was listening to. His lips glistened with saliva and my heart raced as I imagined kissing those lips. The train is not too crowded at that early hour so it was just he and I sitting in that particular section of the train car. I was glad for that, seeing as the conversation I was about to embark upon with him was not really for others to hear. (I mean, how often does a guy talk about his damned socks?) I suppose that even with his eyes closed he sensed me sitting there looking at him because his eyes suddenly came open. He looked over at me looking at him.

"Good morning," I said and he quickly turned down the volume on his portable CD player.

"Good morning," he responded. "Just need to lower this thing."

"It's okay," I said with a smile. "Who are you listening to?"

"TLC, their first album," he replied, taking the earphones from his ears. "Can't get enough of it."

"I see," I said. "I didn't mean to interrupt you; I know you like to doze while riding the train."

I sounded totally awkward and nervous at the same time.

"I've seen you the last couple of weeks and there's a really silly question I would like to ask you," I went on.

"Sure thing," he said and smiled.

Then, to my sudden astonishment he crossed one leg up, his foot now resting on his knee, dangling inches within my reach. God, I could not believe it.

"Where did you buy the sheer socks you're wearing?" I asked him, plunging right in.

For a second he seemed taken aback, glanced at his foot resting on his knee and then looked at me again.

"My socks?" he asked me. "You want to know where I bought my socks?"

As we spoke the train barreled into the next station. The doors opened and more passengers boarded, some of them sitting within earshot of us. The doors closed and the train moved on.

"Yes, well, I really like the style of those sheers you're wearing," I said, lowering my voice at that point. "They go real well with what you're wearing. I've looked and looked like crazy but can't find them anywhere. I've gone to various shoe stores and even male accessory stores. No one seems to have them."

Smiling from ear to ear he seemed to drink me in, seeming to know what I was really after.

"I'll tell you man, I've had people ask me where I've bought shirts, suits, ties," he said, giving his tie a nervous tug. "I've even had guys in the locker room ask me where I had bought my damned underpants, but no one has ever asked me where I bought my socks."

At that we both smiled and laughed softly, both of us glancing down at his foot resting on his knee, his black ribbed sheer sock in full view.

"These are called TNT socks actually," he explained. "That means thick and thins. The toes sections of them are solid black silk and so are the tops of them. The center section, from the middle of the top of the foot to just about the calf is sheer."

My heart was pounding as he spoke and I felt a chub starting in my pants.

"If I were wearing slip-ons I would be able to show you the toes section and what I mean," he went on. "Although I don't feel like taking my shoes off on the train, you know? Even this early in the morning my feet sweat a lot and my socks pretty much smell."

Again we both laughed softly.

"Here, see what I mean," he said and pushed his navy blue dress pants leg up to show me the top of his sheer sock.

It was calf length and yes the topmost part of it was solid black silk. Against his smooth brown skin it looked more than erotic. His mention of how his socks smelled, even this early in the morning was too much for me.

"Nice, real nice," I said, having to restrain myself from reaching out and touching his damned sock.

"But anyway, to answer your question I bought a bunch of pairs of these at a shoe store near where I work," he said to me, not pushing his pants leg back down again. "It's on forty fourth street right off Sixth Avenue."

"I'll have to come uptown after work tonight and check it out," I said, reaching forward, and without even thinking gave his sheer socked ankle a squeeze.

"You work downtown huh?" he asked me with a smile on his handsome face. "I see you get off the train at West Fourth Street."

"I work on Fourteenth Street," I said. "I get off at West Fourth and then walk the few blocks to my building."

"I see," he said. "And with all those stores on Fourteenth Street that cater to Spanish people you couldn't find one that sold sheer socks? I mean, Spanish guys love the style of sheers more than anybody I would think."

"I, uh, guess I didn't look hard enough," I said, trying to sound convincing.

"You're probably just like the salesman in the store who sold me these shoes the day I also bought the sheer socks man," he said to me, moving his sheer socked foot closer to my hand.

"Just like the salesman?" I asked him. "I don't think I understand.

"Well, when I tried the shoes on I found that they were too tight with the regular dress socks I was wearing that day," the handsome black guy said, wagging his foot up and down near my hand. "So when I told the salesman that they felt too tight he suggested that I should change my socks. He suggested the sheers I'm wearing now. I agreed to his suggestion and fuck man, that guy could not take his eyes off my feet as I changed socks. I even apologized for how bad my socks and feet stunk when I had taken my socks off. He just smiled, inhaled deeply and told me that he'd smelled a lot worse than mine in his time."

Listening to this guy talk about his shoe and sock purchasing experience was blowing my mind. I was more than chubbed in my pants listening to him.

"And then," he went on. "After I had gotten the sheer socks on my smelly feet the salesman couldn't get my feet into his lap fast enough so that he could get the shoes on me, slowly. While he shoed my feet my dress socks were on the floor by the chair I was sitting in. I had the distinct goddamned feeling that given the chance he would have snagged my socks. Can you imagine?"

I simply smiled at him and again gave his sheer socked ankle a squeeze.

"So, my thinking was that that shoe salesman had a definite sock and foot fetish," he went on explaining. "So, are you like that salesman bud?"

Before I replied we both glanced down at his foot resting on his knee. By now the train was half crowded, but like most times in New York City nobody seemed to be paying attention to us.

"I, I suppose you could say that man," I said sheepishly.

"I know," he said and grinned real big from ear to ear. "I knew it the first time I saw you bud."

"I don't understand," I said, trying to feign ignorance.

"I've seen you looking at my feet the few times I've seen you here on the train," he said. "Why do you think I stretched them out in front of you those times?"

"But your eyes were always closed," I said.

"Not always," he said, his grin getting wider.

With that he moved his foot off his knee and down to the floor.

"My name is Tyrone," he said, holding his hand out.

"I'm Christopher," I replied, shaking his hand, noticing that both of our palms were sweaty feeling.

"Meet me at the shoe store tonight after work Christopher," he said, practically commandingly. "Say about six fifteen. That should give you enough time to get uptown. I'll help you pick out some sheer socks for yourself."

"Th-thanks," I said and let go of his hand. "I'll be there."

"I know you will," he said and put his headphones back

in his ears. "Nice meeting you Christopher. Or should I say, nice feeting you?"

That said he smiled once more, closed his eyes, leaned back in his seat and got lost in the music he was listening to...

A Bad (Good) Day

What a day it had been. First my computer went down for two hours, setting me back on my work, then one of my company's biggest clients canceled their account with us. My boss chewed me a new asshole for that (for about a half hour or so) because it was my account, my fucking responsibility. And then, on the way home my goddamned train delayed for about ten minutes in a dingy tunnel. I was never so glad to be getting home as I was on that night after work. Dressed in a navy blue suit, a light blue shirt, a red and blue patterned silk necktie, black cap-toe shoes and grey calf length socks (yeah, I had meant to put on blue or black socks that morning but when I had reached into my overly filled sock drawer I was more asleep than awake so I didn't notice that I was wearing grey socks till it was too late) I strolled down my block toward my apartment in Brooklyn, carrying my attaché case. What I didn't know was that my bad day was about to get even worse. When I opened my apartment door and stepped inside I was suddenly grabbed by my tie and hauled roughly forward.

"UNNNFFFF!!!" I gasped and dropped my attaché case on the floor as I was taken totally by surprise.

"Gotcha suit boy!" a big and burly looking guy roared in my face.

He pulled me close to himself, practically lifting me off the floor by my tie.

"WH-WHAT the fuck is this??" I croaked and saw another

guy standing next to the one who had grabbed me. "WH-WHO the fuck are you guys???"

"Work him over Cleeve," the second guy said to the one holding me by my tie, choking the fuck out of me I might add, cutting off my air and voice.

The guy who had me by the tie made a huge fist and punched me hard in the old gut.

"OOOOFFF..." I said as the wind was knocked out of me.

Before I could double over in pain he punched me again and again and again in the stomach, dancing me around the room on my toes as he did so. When he (finally) stopped punching me he pushed me across the room to the other guy (practically flinging me) who caught me in a tight bear hug. I was gasping for breath from all the punches I had just endured as the guy held me close to himself, pinning my arms to my sides in his iron-like grip.

"Cute, real fucking cute," he said and kissed me in a licking and slobbering manner on the side of my neck, just above the collar of my shirt.

"Fucking faggots," I whispered angrily. "I remember you two now..."

I had been at a corporate company gathering a week before where I had hung my suit jacket on the back of my chair at the conference table. My wallet was in the inside pocket of the jacket. The two men in my apartment had been waiters at that gathering and had obviously gotten my address from my wallet while I had excused myself to the men's room. Very stupid of me to have left my wallet unattended. How they had gotten into my apartment will always remain a mystery to me. The second man held me tight in the bear hug and hoisted me a few inches off the floor.

"WH-what the fuck do you guys want, money?" I asked them and they laughed at my question.

"We don't want your money suit boy," the man called Cleeve said to me. "We just want a little fun with you…"

I looked down at the second man and yelled "Put me the fuck down you bastard!!!" at him, hoping also that one of my neighbors would hear me and call the cops, no such luck though, this is New York after all. The two men laughed harder and I struggled in the man's grasp as he lugged me toward my bedroom. Moments later the two bastards had me stripped to my white briefs and those accursed grey socks I mentioned earlier. I was stretched out on my bed on my back with my wrists cuffed above me to the bed board. The two men each took one of my socked feet in their hands and began licking them, sucking on them, sucked my toes, and kiss, kiss, kissing them. I could not believe what I was seeing, and feeling.

"Fucking perverts, sleazy foot faggots!" I roared at them. "Look at you two licking my damned smelly socked feet. What a thing! Is that what the fuck you came here for? To lick an executive's goddamned end of the day rank feet? Shit, I've been wearing those damned socks since before six AM this morning!!"

They licked my feet till my goddamned socks were soaked with their saliva. Then, I watched as they jacked the fuck off all over my chest and licked their slimy cum off me, paying special attention to my tits, really sucking the fucks out of them. They leered at me, tousled my brown wavy hair, licked my stinky armpits, and fucking kissed me all over. All throughout the horrendous ordeal I swore at them like a damned captured sailor.

When they had had enough of me they stripped my briefs off me, uncuffed my hands, and ran out of my apartment like two bats out of hell, my briefs in the first man's hand. Huffing for breath I sat up on the bed, rolled my smelly socks off my feet, pressed them against my nose and mouth, and inhaled deeply. I jacked off as I sniffed the two rapist's saliva on my socks... *What a day it had been...*

About the Author

Christopher Trevor was born in July 1963 and grew up in New York City. As soon as he was old enough to know how he began writing fiction and has been writing gay erotic/fetish stories for the past ten to twelve years at this point. He became an avid reader as well from the time he knew how and reads everything from fiction, to non-fiction to biographies of interesting and unusual people, people who have made a difference or who have paved the way for others. Christopher attributes his writing artistic inspiration to artists such as  Etienne, Tom of Finland, Tagame, The Hun, and most notably Joe T, who Christopher has had the pleasure of speaking with and even meeting over the last few years. Christopher states, "Joe T encouraged me to write about my fetish because I was embarrassed about it at the time. Joe T said that when we are embarrassed about something that makes it even more enticing somehow." Christopher totally agreed and never stopped writing in this genre. Erotic writers who inspired Christopher Trevor were: Tom Shaw (author of "That Day at the Quarry), C.S. White (author of Big Sur), Larry Townsend (author of countless erotic novels), and Mason Powell (author of the classic story "The Brig.")

Christopher discovered that not only did he enjoy writing erotic tales but that after his first bondage experience he had a genuine flair for it. Writing to erotic oriented magazines about his first bondage experience truly opened the floodgates for Christopher where this style of writing is concerned. Christopher thanks the handsome and muscular "Greg" for that experience way back in time. Christopher took "Creative Writing" courses every semester during his high school years and while other friends of his stopped writing what they loved to write about as time went on Christopher never let a day go by when he didn't write something... "I feel that if I don't write every day I will die," Christopher has said many times over.

Foot fetish stories and all things related; spanking fetish, erotic shaving, muscle bondage, tickle torture, and hardcore stories are just a few of the areas of gay eroticism that Christopher enjoys writing about and inspiring in others as well. As one internet buddy said to Christopher where the black socks fetish is concerned, "Until I started talking with you I never gave a thought to my socks when I got dressed for work in the morning. Now when I pull my dress socks on every morning I get a chill up my spine."

Christopher is proud of the erotic effect he has on people...

Christopher Trevor is also the author of:

> **The Executive Guide to Foot Fetishism and Office Discipline**
> 1-887895-36-1

> **Executive Ties That Bind**
> 1-887895-37-X

> **Don't!! Stop!! That Tickles!!**
> 1-887895-31-0

> **The Taming of Dominick**
> 1-887895-45-0

Timmy and The Hong Kong Tailor
1-887895-30-2

Love, Torture and Redemption
1-887895-32-9

Timmys Ticklish Trials
978-1-887895-74-3

Milked
978-1-887895-66-8

Erotic Street Blues
978-1-887895-97-2

Look for them where you found this book or Goodboner.com.

www.ingramcontent.com/pod-product-compliance
Lightning Source LLC
Chambersburg PA
CBHW071223260626
47162CB00004B/1402